Al

MW01135707

A Novel by Greg Vines

Dedicated to my children: Israel – for teaching me to read
and Haley – for being fearless

The events and characters in this book are fictitious.

ISBN: 9781983177095

2nd Edition of All I Ever Seen

No content has changed…only formatting

Chapter 1

That Night in Circle City

Unable to make the migration known as the Great White Flight, their families stayed behind in the decaying inner-city neighborhoods. The men were spiritually calloused and the women were taught to do whatever was necessary to get by. Travis's daddy, James, was mean and bitter. Emasculated during the Korean War, he returned to the states a morphine addict. Once the VA weaned him off the morphine, he turned to alcohol. He drank and worked on cars at home during the day and was a gas station attendant at night. He was abusive of his wife and accused her of infidelity. She didn't bother denying any of it. Once he was big enough, Travis, on the other hand, fought back. He said he was tired of the beatings with the barber's strop and had no intentions of running anymore. They had some real brawls once Travis came of age. Before long, James decided he'd be better off not saying anything when he caught Travis smoking weed or sniffing gasoline.

Mac's old man Horace was an odd sort. Very introverted, Horace appeared, on the surface at least, to be reasonably bright. He worked as a municipal bus driver. Horace not only subscribed to but actually read National Geographic. A sober and God-fearing soul, Horace, without fail, dragged Mac and the other family members to church twice a week. Mac would always disappear to meet Travis, Booger, and the other neighborhood ne'er do wells. They would smoke cigarettes and grope the girls that would allow it. It was at one such Wednesday night church service that Mac met Danielle in an empty room on the upper level of the old church where they both lost their virginity.

Booger's daddy was a municipal water works employee. Hardened during the Great Depression, he learned early to care for himself. He was as adept at carpentry as he was working on cars. Big Daddy (as he was called) made extra money working odd jobs at almost anything. He always provided for his family but never learned how to express his love for them. Booger worshipped and feared his father.

Much like his father, Travis was mean. Booger & Mac thought it was because of the beatings but Travis' issues were much deeper than that. Travis' persona was scarred by fear. Fear of success, fear of failure, fear of dying, and fear of the unknown. He was above average intellectually but purposely sabotaged academic endeavors out of fear that expectations would be placed upon him. Expectations that he could never live up to were Travis' greatest fear. Socially, Travis was looked upon as the guy you didn't want to mess with unless you were a girl with a severely convoluted panache. Many were the young ladies that thought the bad boy personality was all a front and that Travis could be somehow tamed. Few were those that succeeded in bringing out the light in his darkness and once they did, had nothing to do with him.

After his encounter with Danielle in the book depository at the church that night, Mac changed. The others didn't know it, but Mac became a chronic bed wetter. His grades in school dropped and he became something of a thrill seeker. He distanced himself from the others by seeking comfort in heroin and pornography. It was not until later that Mac realized he was a homosexual.

Booger was the court jester, the people pleaser, and the class clown all neatly packaged with a gold ribbon and a helium-filled balloon. Everybody loved Booger. The teachers, the clergy, the girls, the long hairs, and the jocks all loved Booger. Personally, he held little interest in any of them but sought their acceptance as a substitute for his lack of self-esteem. The girls were especially prone to his charm, and despite the broken hearts, they still fell for him time and again. They had known each other for most of their lives. Each thought they knew the others' strengths, weaknesses, fears, fantasies, likes, and dislikes.

It was a foregone conclusion that they would all be drafted into the military. Mac was first. He enrolled in a local community college after he was assigned a 4F deferment. He told Booger it was because he had flat feet but Travis had already figured out that Mac was queer. It didn't matter to Travis. Despite his many transgressions, Travis was in no way prejudiced.

Booger enrolled in school as well. Big Daddy had told him that welding school would be a good trade and keep him out of the draft at the same time. Booger knew that Big

Daddy was ashamed of the fact that he had not served in Korea because of scoliosis and would like nothing more than to live vicariously through his son's service. They never talked openly about it, and Booger knew that welding school would not exempt him from the draft. He was resigned to the fact that he was going to serve but was not so benevolent that he would enlist of his own free will.

Despite the persona of being the consummate tough guy, the notion of being in the military with a license to use firearms and explosives with intent to kill went against Travis' grain for some reason. Any mention of the military, the draft or the conflict in S.E. Asia angered him. Anger, it is said, is a secondary emotion employed to mask fear.

The trip was a sort of last hoorah if you will. Despite having been close all of their lives, the boys instinctively knew that this would soon change, and that separation was to be a part of that change. They had bought a car. That is to say, they had conned old man Cain out of a car with a promise to pay the $75 balance in one week. Mr. Cain worked on, bought and sold, traded, and junked used cars and was not fooled by their plan. He had 1960 Chevy station wagon sitting in the front yard with a For Sale sign in the windshield. Knowing before they ever knocked on the door that these three had a plan up their sleeve, Mr. Cain had already covered his tracks. After some lengthy discourse on the automobile's attributes, he told the boys the car was worth $600 but that he would take $400 for it. They had scraped together $325 for a car and explained that they were going to Florida for work and could pay the balance in one week. Because old man Cain only had $200 in the car so they all agreed to the following terms: Mr. Cain would furnish a bill of sale and registration on the car in exchange for their $325. This put him $125 to the good right out of the chute. Upon receipt of the $75 balance, he would sign the title granting ownership. This was the green light the boys were looking for. They had no intentions of keeping the car. They figured they could sell it and recoup their original $325 AND pay old man Cain his $75 thus getting a free ride for a week. What could go wrong?

They left around mid-day with the intention of missing both the Atlanta traffic and the traffic in Columbus. Once they crossed the Chattahoochee River and drove into Phoenix City, they decided to make a pit stop for beer and boiled peanuts. Confident they would not get carded for beer, they stopped on the outskirts of town at a little mom and pop gas station/convenience store. Travis went in for the beer and Booger pumped the gas while Mac slept on the old twin mattress they had put in the back of the station wagon.

The couple in the pickup truck caught Booger's attention. They were cussing and raising all kinds of hell about something when she jumped out of the truck. She was tearing around the parking lot like a Mexican fighting chicken when the skinny little redneck behind the wheel followed suit. He took one step too many towards her and she raked her nails across his face sending him cowering back to the truck. He cranked the old truck and stirred up a cloud of dust getting out of there, leaving her behind.

Booger shouted, "You alright?"

"What do you care?" She replied.

When Travis came out of the store she was standing there whacking a pack of Marlboro cigarettes against the heel of her hand. She was a special specimen of purebred white trash Travis thought to himself. Her hair was the color of a no longer new penny and reached past her shoulders. She smelled like sun-dried linen sheets. Unless one considers a smattering of freckles on the bridge of the nose a flaw, her complexion was perfect. She had pale green eyes and teeth that were pure white. It was difficult to guess her age. She might have been 15 and she might have been 25. Either way, she was full grown. She wore a pair of cutoff denim shorts and a halter top. The fine hairs on the small of her back were bleached to a corn tassel hue that caught the rays of the afternoon sun.

She had grown up with little supervision save that of her grandparents. Granny and Papa were both textile mill workers. Her mother was as worthless as her brothers. They were a discontented lot that substituted the discipline required to better themselves with anger, resentment, and liquor. There was a parade of men in and out of the trailer they occupied. Some stayed for a while; others did not. She never knew her father. Her mother worked on the killing floor of a poultry processing plant at night leaving her defenseless most of the time. It was in that trailer on a night her mother was working that she nearly lost a struggle with one of her uncles. Having advanced on her, she cut him with a kitchen knife nearly severing his nose. For her actions, she spent the summer of her 12th year in the Russell Co. Juvenile Detention Center. She was disinterested in school but test scores indicated that she was much brighter than her grades indicated. A teacher was once asked the class what they wanted to be when they grew up. "I'd like to be an artist," she replied when it was her turn to speak. A classmate in the back of the room snickered and whispered, "More likely to be a whore like your mama." On the way home from school that day, she stuck a thumbtack into the eraser of a pencil. The tack, having been rubbed vigorously on the sheet metal wall of the school bus, grew exceedingly hot and glowed. Laughing maniacally, she used it to burn the back of her classmate's neck.

Roxanne was haunted by the thoughts of being bound by her circumstance and vowed always to escape. She had a cousin with whom she shared her thoughts and feelings. His name was Henry. Like herself, Henry was inexplicably *different* from members of the Benefield clan. Henry and Roxanne did everything together. They shared ideas, hopes, and fears and swore they would always be there for each other. They had been swimming together one summer day.

Having gotten out of the water, they fell asleep under a shade tree. Once awakened, the two found themselves staring silently at each other. Pulses quickened. Roxanne moved closer and kissed Henry on the mouth. Soon entangled, she gave herself fully to him. Later that day, as they were returning home, an afternoon thunderstorm developed. They took shelter in an old barn where they again submitted to each other. Afterward, Henry, standing naked outside the barn laughing, was struck dead by lightning. He was seventeen years old. Roxanne was fourteen. The next three years were nearly unbearable for Roxanne. She was ridiculed and molested. What others did not blame her for she blamed of herself. It was this soup of discord from which she ran.

"Got a light?" She asked when Travis walked out carrying the peanuts and beer.

"Nah, those damn things make your mouth taste like an ashtray," he replied.

"Jerk," she said. "You'll never know what my mouth tastes like".

Travis continued to walk towards the station wagon. If she wasn't trouble, she was the next best thing Travis thought to himself. Mac was busy flipping the mattress when Travis got back to the station wagon. He grabbed his bag of clothes and headed towards the restroom around the corner of the building. Travis didn't say anything. When Booger came out of the store with the beer, Roxanne gave him a *come-hither* finger wag from the pay phone. Booger walked to the corner of the store and stood obediently while she finished having her temper tantrum with the person on the other end of the phone line. Mid-rant she asked, "You got a light?"

"Sure," Booger said, hurrying back to the store to buy a lighter.

When he returned, she was leaning impatiently against the building with one leg bent at the knee, her foot against the wall. Booger handed her the lighter with the Confederate flag likeness.

She lit her cigarette and asked, "What's your friend's problem?"

Enamored, Booger said, "You just gotta get to know him. He ain't all bad."

"Yeah right," she said.

Watching from the station wagon, Travis grew impatient and cranked the car while sounding the horn. He raced the engine and drove up to the corner of the building where the payphone was located. Oblivious to the happenstance, Mac walked out of the bathroom and got back into the car.

"Are you coming or are you gonna stand there and watch the train wreck?" Travis shouted to Booger.

"Just a second," Booger countered.

"I need a ride to Eufaula," she said.

"Come on," Booger said, holding the rear door open.

"Aw hell no!" Travis yelled.

"I don't know what your problem is, but get over it!" she yelled.

"My problem is I don't like white trash like you that think they can just wag their finger and get what they want."

"Always worked before," she replied with a catty grin.

Booger jumped in. "Look Trav, she just needs a ride to Eufaula. It's just 45 miles. Ok?"

"Whatever."

It was hot and the A/C on the old station wagon didn't work. Scarcely 15 minutes had passed since they left the gas station when she spoke. "What's that smell?"

Travis turned into the rest area. Enraged, he walked to the passenger side of the station wagon and opened the rear door. He grabbed her by the arm.

"Get the hell out!" he shouted.

He dragged her kicking and screaming towards the large building that housed the showers and restrooms. Save for themselves, the rest area was void of any other travelers. Mac and Booger had seen this temperament before and knew better than to engage in any peacemaking efforts. They sat like children waiting for Travis to return. When they came out of the building, Travis walked slowly towards the car. She was two steps behind him. Booger noticed the button on her shorts was undone and her face was flush. Travis' shirt hung limply across his shoulder. She had a disheveled look about her as Travis quietly removed the mattress from the back of the station wagon and left it on the ground next to the dumpster.

"Seems that Roxanne now needs a ride to Circle City," Travis reported.

"They call me Booger and this is Mac."

She slid across the front seat and sat shoulder to shoulder with Travis as they left the rest area.

The Palomino Club was one part strip club, one part biker bar, and one part music venue strategically located on the back side of a small strip shopping center in Circle City. It was the kind of place that refused to sell beer in bottles or serve drinks in anything other than plastic cups for the obvious reason that glass, in the hands of a drunken stripper or biker, became a lethal weapon. Roxanne told them to wait in the station wagon and that she would be right back. Booger's eyes were bugged out and he was sweating profusely. This was not the sort of place that Booger could nice guy his way out of a jam and he knew it. Mac was coming out of his morphine-induced haze he had initiated at the gas station in Phoenix City. He looked around and asked Travis where they were.

"We're in Circle City," Travis said. "We'll be rolling in a minute."

Roxanne came out to the car. The clientele watched from behind the windows that were tinted with spray paint. "Y'all go get a room at that motel down the street. I'll meet you there in a couple of hours."

The lonely sense of separation touched them all when they pulled out of the parking lot. They barely knew her. What they did know was that she was in trouble and that she had drawn them in. There was no getting away from her now. They were bound by poverty, desperation, pride, fear, and an overwhelming need to break free of the chains that tied them to their past and denied them of their future.

Later that night, Travis sat straight up on the bed and gasped. He didn't need a clock on the wall to tell him that something was terribly wrong. It was dark and neither Booger nor Mac was in the room. A quick glance around the small room revealed a note. "Gone to get Roxanne," it read.

"Damnit!" he said under his breath as he darted out of the motel room door. The station wagon was gone, so he started walking. "I knew it," he muttered repeatedly. "We should've left that little tramp at the rest area!" It was a short distance back to the Palomino Club, and when he got there, Travis recalled the last time he saw as many Panheads and Shovelheads lined up at one place and it was NOT a fond memory. At his mother's behest, he'd once gone to retrieve his father from just such a place. There was no happy ending to that story and Travis had feared a similar result this night. His plea to waive the cover charge at the door because he was *just looking for a friend* was met with a drunken laugh. The bouncer was in bad need of dental maintenance and he did reek of gasoline and cigarettes. His fingernails were blackened by timeless grime from who knows where, and the Colt Python in the shoulder rig was a clear indication that this was not a costume party. After handing over the cover charge, Travis stood just inside the door for a minute allowing his eyes to adjust to the dim lighting

There was a crowd around the lone pool table. The patrons were laughing, spilling drinks, and throwing the occasional punch. Travis did not see Roxanne in the room. Booger was at a table in the corner with Mac. They appeared small and scared as they tried to imitate the revelry that their consociates were enjoying. A large hand wrapped itself around Travis' upper arm.

"Your old lady owes us five-hundred dollars," he said.

As he turned to answer, Travis felt the sharp sting of an open hand slap across his face. "I ain't got an old lady," Travis replied.

Travis was escorted to the table where Booger and Mac were sitting and shoved into an empty chair. "Tell it to the man."

Mac had read enough of Horace's National Geographic magazine to know that every baboon tribe was based on a social structure and this tribe's alpha male had just seated himself next to Travis. Travis knew *the man* when he saw him. He was not large in stature. Travis noticed how the veins in his arms bulged and he tried not to fixate on the scar that marked his face.

"You play cards?" he asked.

"No," Travis replied.

"Neither does your old lady!" one of the subordinates shouted. They all laughed until the alpha shot a glance around the table.

"We take poker serious around here," he said. "She knew that when she got in the game."

"What's your point?" Travis replied. Again he felt the sting of the open hand slap across his face. Booger shuddered uncontrollably and Mac pissed his pants.

"Point is she lost $500, and these two clowns said you'd make good on the debt."

"We, I said we would make good on the debt," cried Booger.

"You've got 24 hrs. Just to be safe, I'll hang on to the girl and the car 'til you get back." They walked out and started back towards the motel.

They walked in silence until they got back to the motel, and Booger offered an apology. "I'm Sorry? Sorry ain't gonna save our ass on this one Booger!" Travis shouted.

Mac was staring blankly out of the window in the room that faced the back of the small motel. "What are all those lights and cars over there?" he pondered out loud.

"Who gives a rat's ass Mac?" was Travis' reply.

Mac said, "I'll be back shortly." Travis and Booger looked at each other as though they both had the same question and the same answer. When he returned sometime later, Mac's eyes lit up like lanterns. "I have an idea," he said and smiled

Of all the cockamamie ideas these three ever cooked up, this one actually sounded good. Booger drew the short straw thus becoming the designated sacrificial lamb. Booger, as it turned out, actually had the safest role to play in their scheme. The revival was being held at the fairgrounds. That afternoon, they went to the matinee to get a feel for it all and became convinced they could pull it off. After going over their plan again, they returned for the main service that evening. Mac and Travis took their seats on opposite sides of the arena which was an open-air *shed* used for rodeos, livestock auctions, and concert stage. Booger waited outside in one of the many Port-O-Lets that had been brought in for the revival. The call for donations had been made and the makeshift donation plates (pillow cases) were passed through the fever-pitched throng as the pastor brought the crowd to a riotous level of piety. It was time for the altar call. This was the point in the service when those overcome with guilt, shame, and remorse stepped forward for a dose of salvation. It was also Booger's cue.

Waving his arms, Booger came running through the crowd wearing nothing but his cleanest pair of dirty underwear and a rubber mask that resembled Richard Nixon. "Wash me in the blood of the lamb!" he shouted. After making a couple of laps to the delight of the throng, he ran up on the makeshift stage and jumped into the baptismal which was a galvanized stock tank on loan from the local farm supply dealer. Thrashing about wildly and screaming for salvation, he had drawn fully the attention of all those in attendance. Travis and Mac made their exits. Their pillowcases laden with cash and coin, Travis took the exit to the left and Mac to the right. They were virtually undetected. Booger was left thrashing about in the stock tank. Travis bumped into an old man that was carrying a ram's horn as he exited one of the Port-O-Lets. Travis didn't give it much thought, but this chance encounter turned out to be more serious than they thought. It was the point at which things became quite serious.

Mac and Travis took different paths and met back at the motel. Hurriedly, they counted the folding money to make sure there were adequate funds. The plan was for them to all separate and meet in Phoenix City. Mac went to the bus station and tried to be discreet until the bus arrived. Booger stepped quietly out of the stock tank once the organizers realized what had happened; it would seem they were more concerned with their money than Booger's salvation. Booger left the stage to retrieve the clothes hidden behind the Port-O-Let and changed behind a cargo van parked nearby. Travis left the motel and went back to the Palomino Club. The scene at the club was no different than it was the day before. Travis was escorted to his regular table where he settled Roxanne's debt. He was given the key to the station wagon but before he could get out of the parking lot Roxanne walked in front of the car yelling, "You ain't leaving without me you sonofabitch!" He swerved around her, and the tires squealed on the incline when he left the parking lot. A county deputy that had been working off-duty at the revival came into the club parking area from the other end. Roxanne was still in the parking lot pitching a fit. She was drunk and disheveled, and that was more than enough cause for the deputy to stop and investigate. She had no ID but the deputy had no reason to think she might be lying about her age. It was the commotion he was concerned with. He got her seated in the back of the car and walked into the club. He was familiar with the club and most of its patrons, and his presence was as familiar to them.

"Who's the redhead raising hell in the parking lot?"

"Walked in here yesterday looking for a good time," was the reply. It was while they were all laughing that the deputy noticed the pillowcase.

"Where did that come from?" he asked. "The bedroom," replied one of the subordinate tribe members.

He didn't find the ensuing round of laughter entertaining and grabbed one of the revelers by his arm. Before any further chaos could emanate, the alpha walked up. "What's the problem, deputy?" They knew each other. They were both from the same area. One was from one side of the tracks and one from the other.

"Problem is, there was a bit of a disturbance at the revival and some money turned up missing. Money that had been collected in a pillowcase."

"I wouldn't know much about a revival but I can explain the pillowcase. Come on over."

The two went to an empty table. The tribe had nothing to hide and certainly had no concern for Roxanne or her compadres. The whole story was recounted to the deputy. The story of the card game, a description of the other suspects, and a description of the station wagon were tied up nice and neat with a ribbon and a bow and handed to the deputy. Having already picked out the folding money and counting out the $500 owed, the leader handed the pillowcase laden with coins of various denominations to the deputy. The deputy returned to the car and radioed the office. Roxanne had passed out in the backseat. He took her back to the jail to be held until she sobered up. The surrounding five counties were all notified of what had happened and the search began. The charges pending were manslaughter and theft by taking. It seems that the old man that Travis bumped into had fallen. The tip of the ram's horn slipped between two ribs and pierced his lung. Lying on the sawdust-covered fairground, the old man drowned in his own blood.

Mac grew irritable. His muscles began to cramp and he was sweating profusely. In his haste at the motel, he'd left what little dope he had. Normally, he would go to the local country doctor to initiate the ploy designed to convince the doctor that he was suffering from a kidney stone. His body temperature already elevated, the palpable discomfort usually convinced the doctor. When asked for a urine sample, Mac would prick his finger and squeeze a drop of blood into the specimen cup. This eliminated all doubt and he was given Dilaudid for pain. The Dilaudid metabolized into morphine once injected and all was well. This, however, was a rather precarious situation. It was after hours and there was no doctor to con.

Mac watched a young Marine walk toward the bathroom. He was gone for quite some time, and when he returned, he sat nodding and rubbing his nose incessantly. Mac recognized the symptoms. When the soldier cast a lascivious look in Mac's direction, Mac knew all too well that his pain would soon end. He smiled and headed to the men's' room to wait in the lone stall. The Marine came in after placing an Out of Order notice on the entry door. Mac sat there with his belt wrapped around his arm as his pale-eyed friend prepared what Mac needed. The routine exchange of sexual favor never took place. The heroin was purer than Mac was used to and he was quickly overcome. He fell off the toilet onto the cold tile floor. The soldier unscrewed the sole light bulb on his way out and returned to the main terminal to find his bus being boarded. He took his place in line. The vision of Mac on the bathroom floor quickly faded. The collage of atrocities he'd witnessed during his tour of Vietnam was far more disconcerting. Mac, after all, was a willing participant in his own demise. By the time the terminal manager had gone to check the restroom at the behest of a number of men needing to use the facility, Mac was as cold as the tile floor which he lay upon. His respiratory system had slowed to a level that would no longer sustain him, and he expired having never known the answers to the questions he'd only asked himself and none other. Among his few belongings was the handwritten Bill of Sale and registration for the station wagon and a picture of Danielle. His clothes were in one of the pillowcases that had been used as a collection plate. Although tragic, Mac's demise most likely precluded the many hardships that a soul of his nature might have encountered. His 4F deferment and his effeminate attributes would make things extremely difficult for him. Even Mac knew this. It was the cause of his death. The overdose was merely a vehicle. It was a way to avert having to come to terms with his place in the world.

Booger had gone to a truck stop where he hitched a ride with a trucker out of Florida. The chatter on the CB radio horrified Booger. News of what had happened in Circle City was rampant and traveled unencumbered by the radio transmissions. He listened quietly to the telling of the Bill of Sale found with the body at the bus terminal and the description of the station wagon. The truckers were laughing uncontrollably when they heard the tale of the guy in his underwear and the rubber mask. It wasn't until the trucker was stopped for a roadside inspection that it became evident that the declaration of *produce* on the driver's manifest had more than a smidgeon of latitude in it. The driver's logs were not current, and the trailer's required annual inspection was expired. When they broke the seal and opened the trailer, they discovered the contraband. Booger pleaded with the Public Safety officers but was held along with the driver until local law enforcement arrived. The two were taken to the county jail and the rig was impounded for evidence. When they searched the cab of the Kenworth tractor they found a paper bag with a pair of dirty underwear and a rubber mask that likened Richard Nixon.

Rather than travel north on 431 to the rendezvous point, Travis had headed east to Georgia. He took State Hwy 52 to State Hwy 62 then got on US 27 North in Blakely, Ga. completely unaware of the impasse that had befallen his friends. The words of his father repeated themselves. "Get used to working boy, you're too damn dumb to steal and get away with it." Just outside of Cuthbert, the Georgia State Patrol officer turned his lights as the blue station wagon passed. He'd heard the vehicle description on the radio, and despite the fact that he was technically off duty, he pulled Travis over to the shoulder. The license plate was verified. The VIN was read back to the dispatcher on duty and he confirmed that it matched the VIN on the registration found with Mac. Travis was taken into custody. He was read his rights. When he heard the charges he hung his head. Monday morning he was extradited back to Alabama and held without bond until the rest of the puzzle was assembled.

Mr. Cain and Horace made the trip to Circle City together. One made the trip to identify the body of his son and the other to stake claim to an automobile. Both men were stoic by nature, and having endured many personal hardships, they had grown calloused and lacked the ability to adequately express their feelings. They rode mostly in silence, each knowing that the others thoughts were similar to their own.

The two men presented themselves at the Sheriff's office and produced the required identification. Horace was escorted to the coroner's office to identify his son's body, and Mr. Cain was led to the impound yard to claim his vehicle. Once their tasks were complete, they ate in silence before the return journey home.

It began to rain just prior to their departure. Halfway to Eufaula, Horace saw the rear of the station wagon waggle ever so slightly before swaying violently in the other direction. The blue station wagon then pitched and went into a roll before coming to rest in a peanut field adjacent to Hwy 431. Horace pulled over and saw that Mr. Cain's body hung still and lifeless from the windshield of the car. Horace stood in the rain. A dog barked. The porch light on the distant farmhouse came on. Horace declined to wait inside for the State Patrol to arrive but rather stood silently in the diminishing rain and waited. For the second time in twenty-four hours, Horace found himself at the Houston Co. Coroner's Office to identify a body. Later, he sat cold and wet in a cheap motel room. Too tired to think, he gazed out the small window at the bright lights of the fairground and the parade of cars coming and going.

For James, there was no epiphany associated with the news of Travis' incarceration. Rather, he was somewhat smug in his vision of Travis as worthless. Somehow it made him feel better about himself. James made the trip to Circle City to gloat rather than to assure his son's care and defense were adequate. He told Travis to write his mother and to make the most of what lay ahead. He assured him that life was composed mostly of hardships and disappointment and that his best bet was to keep his head down and his mouth shut. Travis peered at his father and for a moment actually believed what he was saying before coming to his senses. It was at that moment that Travis cast off the chains of his past. He realized that his belief system to that point in his life had been distorted. His beliefs had been adopted from what others believed to be true. The clarity that came from discarding the beliefs of others and adopting his own was a gift to be revered. In the weeks following the meeting with his father, Travis took stock of his life. He looked at his fears, his regrets, his hopes, and his dreams. He looked at his part in the mistakes he'd made, the people he had harmed, what he truly believed, and what he did not believe. Travis let go of his resentments and antiquated beliefs and was made free. When the judicial system offered to forego the charges against him in return for serving in the armed forces, Travis was grateful and embraced the opportunity to be of service.

He would leave for Pariss Island, SC full of hope and the anticipation of a life filled with purpose. He asked one appeasement of the court. He asked that he be allowed to meet briefly with both Booger and Roxanne before leaving. The judge was reluctant but saw no real harm in his request as long as it was in a supervised setting. Travis told the two of them of his awakening. He admonished at length the freedom he had gained from the realizations he'd come to after meeting with his father. Travis assured Booger that he would write him at his parent's address and asked that he do the same. He forgave Booger for the lies he had told the prosecution, and he forgave him for the *post-mortem* crucifixion of their dead friend. Booger had learned of Mac's passing and used it as a vehicle to assure his own freedom during questioning. He had told the prosecution that it was all Mac's idea and that he was threatened by both Mac and Travis if he did not cooperate in their scheme. Booger was both relieved and ashamed by Travis' benevolence and wept uncontrollably.

Travis turned to Roxanne and took her hand. She had a cut lip and bruises on her upper arms from being grasped while repeatedly struggling with the detention officers. He leaned over and whispered in her ear. She began to cry and nodded her head in agreement. She had no intentions of returning to that mobile home occupied by her whore of a mother. Instead, her mind's eye cast a backward glance at the talc-like red dust that coated the leaves of the plum bushes. She smiled as she recalled the hours she had spent stripping the fruit from those branches and eating the plums with a salt shaker in tow. She remembered the blackberry bushes along the fence rows and storm ditches of the road and smiled as she thought of picking blackberries with her grandmother and of the chigger bites that were the price paid for the pies cooling in the kitchen. She saw a sky so blue that it hurt her eyes and blinded all thoughts of the ridicule and incest and lack of self-esteem she had endured. For the first time in her life, she felt assured that everything was going to be alright and she smiled.

Chapter 2

Charlie and Cynthia Hardwick

Save one, all matters regarding the disturbances that night had been resolved. Charlie Hardwick was the public defender charged with the task of determining what was to become of me. I had no identification and the court was reluctant to believe anything I said. Charlie explained that he would order a Certificate of Live Birth from the Dept. of Vital Records based on the information I had provided. Until the information regarding my age was obtained, I would be held in protective custody by the Dept. of Social Services.

"I can't stay in one of those places. I'll die or kill somebody," I said.

"It's just for a few days," Charlie assured me. "I'll help you get things sorted out when we get the birth certificate."

Charlie was kind and I had begun to trust that he had my best interest at hand. After all, I had little choice. Housing was provided by way of wood framed bivouacs. The white paint curled and split to escape the surface of the pine siding. A large ventilation fan hummed in its housing at the end of the dormitory. The sheets on the steel framed cots were clean. Meals were austere at best, and baloney sandwiches with Kool-Aid were the fare most likely to be served. Once my resolve was tested, and after the fat girl was removed for first aid, the others left me alone. I pondered what lay ahead with quieted resolve.

Charlie Hardwick and his wife Cynthia were natives. Their families had lived in, farmed, invested in, educated their children, and called Dothan, Alabama home since the early 1800s. Charlie and Cynthia held to what they had been taught and questioned not the counsel of their upbringing. They were respected in the community and were sought for advice on matters ranging from business dealings to social etiquette. In the hours of solitude when questions are asked only of oneself, Charlie and Cynthia both had misgivings they never discussed. It somehow seemed blasphemous. They collectively celebrated what others viewed as their successes with little satisfaction.

Their only child had drowned while swimming with friends. Charlie and Cynthia blamed themselves for not being more resolute in their disapproval of Jessica swimming in the river. Jessica did revel in her time with friends in the outdoors. During the hot summer months, she and her friends would refresh in the flow of the west fork of the Choctawhatchee River. There was a spirit in Jessica as wild as the cool green water that eroded small caves into the soapstone bluffs along the river. It was in one such cave that she became disoriented and ultimately struck her head before slipping silently into the water that tumbled along its course to the Choctawhatchee Bay along the panhandle of Florida. They could no more have controlled what happened that day than the events that brought Roxanne into their lives, yet they could not forgive themselves. Cynthia was particularly marked by Jessica's demise. The medication prescribed by Dr. Manor dulled the senses but nothing more.

Charlie:

I received a phone call from the Department of Vital Records when the birth certificate became available. Roxanne was seventeen years old. It took little more investigation to find that she was a high school dropout and a ward of the state as well. I went to see Roxanne and explained that her options were limited at best. She took my hand and thanked me for all that I had done. She stared into my soul with pale green eyes.

"I'll be alright," she said.

I was uncertain of what I felt on the way home. She seemed content. I felt emptiness like no other. I was strangely envious of Roxanne. For no particular reason, I felt compelled to tell Cynthia about Roxanne. I rarely spoke of my work in the courts but this was somehow different. I told her of the circumstances surrounding our acquaintance and the details of her detainment and of the revelations of the records of her life.

"Why are you telling me this?" Cynthia asked.

"I'm not entirely sure."

"Jessica would've been seventeen," Cynthia said. She got up from the table and went out to sit on the porch.

Our home was the same as my father's. Once a working farm, the livestock was now more a diversion and an expense than a capital venture. I enjoyed working with cows. Mowing hay was not to my liking. The fescue grass grew dense in the sandy loam soil. Twice during the summer, Bill Danbury would mow, rake, and bale the hay. I kept half and he took the other. It was a worthwhile arrangement. Each spring during the calving season, I would employ the help of local boys to gather the cattle in a temporary corral with a head catch. One by one the cattle made their way through the structure. Inoculations and routine husbandry completed, they returned to the pastures. I replaced the split rail cedar fence posts as needed and made sure the banks of the small pond were kept relatively clear lest the snakes become too plentiful. I enjoyed fishing for bluegills and bass, and I found it nearly impossible to refuse access to anyone who asked permission to fish. The front porch of our home extended the width of the structure and faced west. The sun had begun to set and a waxing Gibbous moon was rising when I walked outside. Cynthia sat quietly as she often did.

"I'd like to meet her," she said.

The following day, I arranged to visit Roxanne. Cynthia and I drove out to the Department of Social Services and I introduced Cynthia to Roxanne.

"I'd like to speak with Roxanne alone," Cynthia said.

Roxanne smiled at me and nodded her head in approval. They spoke for quite some time. I heard laughter. I saw Roxanne holding Cynthia's hands as she wept. Roxanne smiled and listened.

"We are all exactly where we are supposed to be doing exactly what we're supposed to be doing," Roxanne said. "The things you are told are yours to believe or not. The things that others tell you are their reality. There are no coincidences." Cynthia looked somewhat confused but took solace.

"What will become of her?" Cynthia asked when she came back to the lobby.

"She'll be held until she's of age and then she'll be on her own."

"Hardly seems fair," Cynthia said.

"What's not fair?" I asked.

"None of it is fair. What about guardianship?" she asked.

"I would posit that to be unlikely. She's old beyond her years. It's hard to tell which part of her is real and which is not. If she's not trouble, she's the next best thing to it," I replied

"Charlie Hardwick! All that child needs is a chance to find her footing and you won't help?!"

"Me? What the hell are you talking about?"

"I'm talking about extending a helping hand to a young woman in need. I'm talking about giving her a chance to get her bearings and chart a course."

"She's not a stray dog, Cynthia," I replied.

"That's right, she's not. She's a human being."

"That's a slippery slope, Cynthia. Are you sure?"

"I'm sure I won't forgive myself if I don't."

I went back to see Roxanne the next day. We spoke not of her past but of her future. She spoke of her dreams and desires and of her aspirations. Roxanne painted a canvas of hope and contentment. She spoke of a short list of things that were important to her.

"What about education, family, and a career?" I was embarrassed as soon as the words crossed my lips. These were certainly not the matters of her heart and seemed silly even to me at the moment.

"We're very different people Charlie Hardwick. I can't be bound by the same beliefs that you and Cynthia share. If you're willing to accept that I'd appreciate the help."

"You'll have to finish school, Roxanne. We won't waver on that point," I noted.

"Ok, Charlie," she replied.

It took much longer than he originally thought, but once Charlie had legitimized everything, I was dismissed from the Department of Social Services. I made a point to apologize to the fat girl for breaking her nose.

"Screw you," she said.

"I don't think she believed my sincerity," I thought to myself and smiled. Charlie and I left. He seemed a little nervous being alone with me in the car. I was surprised Cynthia didn't come.

"She's busy getting things ready," he explained.

It was a forty-five-minute drive to the Hardwick family home outside of Dothan. Small talk was sparse and laborious. Charlie was more focused on explaining all of the particulars of the guardianship arrangement, the school board requirements for admissions testing, the rules of the house, and so forth. I politely nodded and occasionally replied in kind with a polite "I see" or "uh huh" to keep things moving along. Charlie was somewhat taken aback when I asked him what was important to him. He began to dissertate on the responsibilities of his job as Public Defender, his commitments to the church and community, and meeting the expectations of others.

"Did you not understand what I asked you, Charlie?" I said shaking my head.

"Of course I did," he replied.

"Well, maybe you'll tell me more someday," I said.

"Of course," he smiled proudly.

We turned off of the highway and onto the county maintained gravel road that led to the Hardwick property. "My great-grandfather planted those pecan trees," Charlie said. "Those trees put me through law school."

"They're beautiful," I said. "The state tree of Texas, I believe."

A pond was situated on the other side of the pecan grove and was fed by a spring nearby. A well house situated close to the main house had drawn water from the aquifer below for over a century. The barn was of cedar and had acquired a silver patina that spoke to its age. There was an old Farmall tractor and a newer Ford under the open overhang of one end of the structure. A number of gently used implements resided there as well. Cynthia waved when we drove up. She had indeed been busy. The *yard,* as it were, was hard packed sand freshly swept clean with a bresh broom. There was an old concrete table with benches akin to those you might see outside of an old church where dinner on the grounds would be served. A pitcher of sun brewed tea, three glasses, and a bucket of ice stood ready. An old tire swing hung silently from the limb of a live oak nearby. It was like no place I'd ever seen.

"Sit. You must be tired," Cynthia smiled.

"I've never had anyone offer me much that didn't come with a string tied to it. I want you to know that I appreciate what you're doing. I've no place to go but much that I want to see and do. I've just got to get myself in position to do it," I explained.

"Roxane, that's true of most anybody. You're no different," Cynthia replied. Charlie nodded his head in agreement.

"I've been largely on my own for quite some time. I've done things I had to do that I'm not proud of. I'm sure my views are very different from yours and if this doesn't work out I understand."

"Did Charlie talk to you about finishing school, Roxanne?" Cynthia inquired.

"He did. I think that's good advice. I just haven't had a chance to get around to it. It seems that just getting by was a full-time occupation that left little time for anything else."

"We'll go over to the school board Monday. I have a friend there that will walk us through the particulars," said Charlie.

"There's one thing that has troubled me since we met, Cynthia," I said.

"What's that?"

"I can't be Jessica. Nobody can. I'd be a fool to try and you and Charlie need to know that. I've got a lot of living to do and right, wrong, good, bad, or indifferent, I intend to do it my way. I don't mean to sound hurtful. Jessica sounds like she was probably a lot like me in some ways but I'd not expect you to be someone you're not and hope you'll afford me the same."

We sat quietly for a minute and drank our tea. "Push me on the swing, Cynthia?"

"You bet," she said.

Charlie went inside. Cynthia and I stayed out until the lightning bugs started to come out. "We'll go get you some clothes tomorrow. Maybe even get our hair and nails done."

"Can I ask you something, Cynthia?"

"Sure," she said.

"What's important to you? Right here, right now, what do you hold closest to your heart?"

"That's a very grown-up question. I'd have to put some thought into it."

"I think about it a lot," I replied

"Come on. I'll show you to your room," Cynthia said.

We walked around the side of the barn to a set of stairs that led to the upper level. Cynthia opened the oddly ornate stained glass door that led to the inside.

"This was Charlie's place when we were young. This is where we courted," she blushed.

It was a large open space. Brass light fixtures hung from the exposed cedar beams of the barn's roof. The heart pine floors were conspicuously clean and lent a warm glow. There was a wood burning stove in the middle of the living area that was vented through the roof. A large braided rug sat beneath an overstuffed sofa and a matching club chair. An old steamer trunk served as a coffee table. A backgammon game sat unfinished. Next to the sofa was an old guitar case. The brass plate on it read CF Martin Co. One wall housed the makings of a small kitchen. Cabinets constructed of wooden crates and chicken wire held a few dishes and drinking glasses. The bedroom was an open space that had been partitioned off by some large bookcases that housed a menagerie of articles. Old photographs, books, a pocket watch, a men's fedora hat, and an old taxidermy mount of a raccoon whispered hints of a time passed. Bare plumbing fed a claw foot bathtub and toilet both modestly camouflaged by dressing screens covered in tapestry. I had never seen anything so beautiful in my life. I fell into the leather sofa and cried. I have no memory of ever crying like that before or since.

Cynthia whispered, "Here and now I hold the joy of doing for you what you cannot do for yourself close to my heart."

Cynthia:

We went shopping the next day. The child had no clothes. She seemed uncomfortable and mildly irritated.

"What's the problem?" I asked.

"I've never had my own room. My clothes came from churches and thrift stores. I'll be gone one day," Roxanne said.

"Don't worry, we'll make sure you pay us back for the clothes and work for your room and board. That way we'll be on even ground."

The arrangement seemed to please Roxanne. Fitting her with clothes was a little trying to say the least. Her butt filled out the seat of the jeans yet her tiny waist and flat belly afforded a gap at the waistband. Long legs made length difficult and shirts that accommodated her more than adequate bust line came with sleeves that were too long.

After a couple of pairs of jeans, a handful of shirts, and some sneakers, Roxanne grew restless. She shook her head when I started going through skirts and dresses.

"Well, let's get some delicates and we'll call it done for now."

"Delicates?" Roxanne inquired.

"Underwear."

We had lunch at the diner in town. When we walked out, Roxanne noticed an old man sitting alone on a bench outside of a barber's shop. Despite the warm weather, the old man was dressed in a long-sleeved shirt and overalls. Brogans on his feet and a Circle City Feed and Seed cap on his head, he was not unlike any one of a number of old men in town. His name was Tom Gentry.

"I'll be right back," Roxanne said. She walked over to the old man and sat down beside him. She gazed into the old man's eyes and took in all that he said. When she spoke, the old man was equally attentive. They laughed out loud there on the sidewalk and it was hard to tell who enjoyed the conversation more. I waited patiently and wondered what they both found so entertaining. After a long while, Roxanne stood up to leave. The old man rose and she hugged him.

"Did you make a new friend, Roxanne?"

"I did. He told me about the things he wished he had done when he was younger and about the things he wished he hadn't done. He told me not to look back on the bad things life throws my way and to forgive those that might wrong me. He told me that resentments never hurt those they are held for but do hurt those that hold them. He said that love can sometimes be likened to a star shower. Bright and beautiful but soon passed. Never be afraid to love just because it might hurt one day," she recounted.

We went to the salon. I was well past needing to do something with my hair. Lorraine would wash, cut and color as usual. Meanwhile, Ty and Ginger attended Roxanne.

"Cynthia, this child has the most beautiful hair I've ever seen. I wouldn't dare cut it, color it, or straighten it. Maybe just a wash and trim," Ty said. "Roxanne?"

"Ok."

I told Ty I'd let my hair air dry and excused myself from the hum of the hair dryers and the mindless blather of the women in the salon. I walked outside and stood alone with my thoughts for a moment. A dog walked up and sat at my feet wagging his tail and looking up at me with big brown eyes. "Well hello, handsome," I said. It was at that time that a girl my age came up.

"Chopper! Where have you been?" "I'm so sorry. He's such a pest," the stranger exclaimed

"Not at all," I replied.

"My name is Collette," she said.

"Roxanne," I replied.

It occurred to me at that moment that no one here had much knowledge of me and thus no preconceived notions of what or who I was or should be. My palette was full and my canvas empty. I could be who I was meant to be instead of what others perceived. That she and I had much in common would be incredulous. I would guess that she had led a very sheltered life, and her notion of a life well lived was filled with visions of a husband, kids, and a career in nursing.

Genuinely kind, she gave me her phone number and asked that I call her. I held that big dumb dog's head in my hands as he licked my face with a canine smile and they left.

When we returned home, Charlie and his Saturday foursome were mildly inebriated and smoking cigars. They were seated in the den playing poker. I pulled up a chair next to Charlie and took stock of the table. The two before him checked.

"Raise Charlie," I said. Charlie looked at me quizzically. "Raise."

"Ok," he finally replied.

The man next to Charlie folded. The remaining two checked back to Charlie.

"Raise again." I insisted.

"Roxanne!" he exclaimed

"You're ok. Trust me".

The player to his right laughed and made light of a kid telling Charlie how to play poker.

"Who do you think you are anyway?" asked the player.

"Looks like I'm the only one here that knows how to play poker," I laughed. "I know what Charlie has and I know what y'all have, so we'll bet the house limit" I stated boldly.

"How the hell do you know what we have?" the player inquired.

"Let's see. You were looking for the third 4 but forgot that this guy over here folded one already. Charlie is holding the other. This guy drew his second pair but it'll never beat our hand. So, like I said, we'll bet the limit." They laughed at each other and folded as Charlie took the pot.

One of the players gestured, "Pull up a chair young lady."

"No thanks guys, I think I'll go read for a while."

Cynthia looked envious when I came back into the kitchen. "We'll grill out later. I'll come up and get you," she said.

Chapter 3

The Party At The Pond

I retired to the barn and took a few books from the shelf. I started reading but soon fell asleep on the leather couch and began to dream.

I had clambered up an embankment that was mostly covered in kudzu. When I got to the top, I found an old roadside sign hanging by but one lone nail on a cedar post. It read: "Retribution for Man's Transgressions Shall Be Swift and Merciless." At the foot of the post, lying dead on the ground was a blue parakeet with ants cavorting in and out of the lifeless eye sockets. It was difficult to take my eyes off of the bird as I continued to walk into the pines. A short distance away, the earth fell off into a large hole. Granite cliffs gave way to a large pool of clear water some sixty feet below. Beneath the water's surface, on the bottom of the great pool of water, I could see a rusted automobile. On the ground a few feet from where I stood, I saw a child's toy. It was a bright yellow bulldozer made of metal. It appeared to be new. As I returned to Granny and Papa's house it began to snow. A large black cauldron filled with water was boiling over a fire near the barn. Pacing about the cauldron were three large, black dogs with yellow eyes. I went inside where we ate fresh biscuits with butter and syrup. Later, I walked outside into the bright night and saw a man in a union suit sitting next to the fire. I walked ever so quietly towards him. The dogs rose and their hair stood up as they growled. The man wore dark glasses and appeared to be blind. His bald head was fully tattooed and I could see that his hands and bare feet were as well. I stood silently and watched him. He had a pad of paper and a pencil and was writing indiscriminately. Papa walked up behind me and whispered, "Beware of darkness child. Just because one does not believe does not mean it ain't so."

"What's he doing Papa?" I asked.

"He's channeling," Papa replied

"Is he a wraith?" I asked. I turned and Papa was not there. The blind man was gone as well. In his stead, a lone child stood crying.

"What's the matter?" I asked.

"The others all make fun of me. They say I'm different."

"Who does?"

"Them," she pointed towards the back of the barn. A small assemblage had gathered and was laughing and pointing at the child. I walked closer. They were a mutant lot. One had scale-like skin and no hair or fingernails. Another's hair was as fine metallic wire and was unable to keep its tongue in its mouth. The two conjoined at the hip stood naked and laughed hysterically. One was black. One was white. I walked back to the child to console her. I explained that being different was something to be proud of. She asked why the others laughed at her.

"They laugh because they are happy for you. They are happy that you are not like them."

When I woke, my heart was pounding. It had grown dark, and in the twilight before awakening, I felt as though I was being watched. Suddenly, a slab of warm, wet flesh swept across my face followed by laughter. I bolted upright only to be eye to eye with a somewhat familiar face. It was Chopper, whom I had met earlier in town.

"You gonna sleep all night?" asked Collette. "Come on. The others are waiting to eat."

"What are you doing here?" I asked.

"My dad plays golf with Mr. Hardwick. We cook out here almost every week. I'll introduce you to some friends."

Some of Charlie's weekly foursome had kids that were mostly of my age. The gathering was a little uncomfortable at first. I felt as though it was supposed to be some sort of "coming out" party in my honor but soon realized that it was not the case. Collette introduced me to her friends as we made our way around the grill. I had never had many friends and was not really sure how or where I was going to fit in or if I even wanted to. They were all nice enough. It was just a little foreign to me. As the adults got mildly inebriated, Collette suggested that we get out for some fun of our own.

"We're gonna go, mom," she said.

"Can I go mom?" her younger sister shouted.

"No ma'am," was the short reply.

"Stay out of that damn river," her father shouted.

Collette promised we would and we all piled into Rory's jeep. Rory was a year older than the rest of us and had graduated from high school the previous spring. The jeep was a present from his parents. Collette and Patti got in the back seat and I conveniently would up front with Rory. As soon as we reached the paved road, Collette lit a joint and started to pass it around.

"Here. Try some Whigham Whamo," she said, passing it over my shoulder.

I took a long draw off the joint. Coughing uncontrollably I said, "Where in God's name did that come from?"

"Whigham, Ga of course! Where else would Whigham Whamo come from?" Patti laughed.

By the time it had made its way around the jeep a couple of times, the resin rich joint had gone out and we were all laughing like hyenas and drinking the Boones Farm wine that Rory had stopped and gotten at the local gas station. We drove around listening to music for a while before Rory pulled off the road. He opened a cattle gate and we started out into a pasture after closing it behind us. Several hundred yards away, the dirt path led through a stand of longleaf pines before coming to a clearing by a large pond. There was a wooden dock with a diving board at the water's edge. No one seemed particularly intrigued by those that were naked. Those in attendance were the long-haired privileged kids of the local liberals. There wasn't one among them that had ever had to fight off so much as a cold I thought to myself. Collette had seemingly disappeared and Patti took my hand. "Come on. We'll walk down to the pond." We stopped along the way to talk to people and never actually made it to the pond.

I wandered off alone and soon came upon Rory and some friends. I stopped and he introduced me around. "Roxanne is staying at the Hardwick's for a while," he told them.

"We heard," one of the boys said. "Good people the Hardwicks." "You're the badass white girl that got in that shit storm at the Palomino Club?" another asked. I immediately felt defensive.

"Hey look, guys, I'm no saint. I come from a not so pretty place with some not so nice people. I've done what I had to do."

It was now apparent that my anonymity was not quite as intact as I had led myself to believe. There had been some talk of who I was and how I wound up here but I didn't know what had been said. I felt obliged to tell them of how I had come to be in their midst. I told them of that night in Circle City as they listened intently. Everyone had heard of what happened at the fairgrounds and of the boy found dead at the bus station but the picture took on a new face of transparency hearing it first-hand. I had filled in the blanks. It had a very sobering effect on them.

Rory took my hand and remarked, "That was quite a tale, Roxanne."

"Look, Rory. I'm not out to impress anybody with wild stories about all of the stuff I've been through. I'm not looking for pity or charity. I can't be anything other than what I am and whether that pleases you or anybody else is secondary," I stated.

"No need in getting pissy, Roxanne! Just give us a chance. Yeah, we're mostly a bunch of rich kids and you're not, but we're pretty open-minded. Friendship and loyalty is held in high regard around here," Rory said defensively

I felt both relieved and apprehensive. I wasn't sure if I was being patronized or pitied. Was I the shiny new toy on the playground or something to make fun of? My apprehension diminished during the course of the evening. Turns out I was pretty good at badminton which the stoners loved to play and I kicked everyone's butt pitching horseshoes. Eventually, someone asked what I thought about the loft in the barn. It was an easy topic and I was able to open up and join the flow of things. As the night wore on, the congregation's topics became more personal. Some spoke of their hopes, others spoke of their fears, many spoke of their opinions.

"What about you?" Collette asked, looking at me. "What do you have planned, Roxanne?"

"I plan to not sit still very long. I'd like to see the country while I'm young."

"You sound just like Jessica. She was part gypsy and part hobo," Collette laughed.

"Maybe so. I just don't want my feet tied to the ground. Not right now anyway," I said.

We were all pretty high at this point, and it was getting late. Some of those in attendance had fallen asleep in lawn chairs while others retired to tents. We rode back to the Hardwick's and crept upstairs to the loft. Patti slept on the couch and Rory on the club chair. Collette and I shared the bed. She held me and began to cry.

"What's the matter?" I asked

"I hope you get to do all that Jessica was only able to dream of, Roxanne," Collette said soberly.

Dr. Richard Pettimore had taken a position at the school board when he retired from teaching law at The University of Alabama. He was a portly gentleman who favored seersucker suits and suspenders, and he was of the belief that a man was never properly dressed until he donned his hat. Being that it was summer, he had appropriately chosen a fine Montecristo straw with a teardrop crown and pinch front. Charlie and I met him for breakfast that morning. Charlie went to work while Dr. Pettimore and I returned to his office to discuss my education or lack thereof.

"Charlie tells me you dropped out of school. Is that correct?"

"I quit going if that's what you mean. I was bored with school and just getting by had become quite a job. I didn't get along very well with the teachers and not much better with the others in my classes," I explained.

"Hmmm. Bored huh? Tell me, Roxanne, what was the last book you read?"

"I read Moby Dick yesterday," was my reply.

"All of it?" Dr. Pettimore asked, raising his eyebrows.

"Yes, sir. I'd read it before."

"Why would you find a whaling story so appealing that you would want to re-read it?" he demanded.

I laughed, "Moby Dick wasn't entirely about whaling, Dr. Pettimore!" I had replied

"Oh? Well what else was it about then?" he inquired

"It was mostly about the struggle between good and evil and the desire to dominate that which cannot be dominated," I replied.

"Why that's preposterous!" Dr. Pettimore exclaimed.

"I beg to differ. Consider why Capt. Ahab was always described as wearing black. Narrative prose has always used the color black to symbolize evil. Moby Dick, however, is depicted as *the great white whale,*" I observed.

Dr. Pettimore seemed taken aback and just short of being embarrassed. "Of course, that's just my interpretation Dr. Pettimore. I'm quite sure that Mr. Melville's detailed accounting of the whaling trade, maritime life, and how to tie a proper knot in a length of rope are all accurate. They're just not of particular interest to me."

"Well, I can see where a man's perspective might be different from a woman's," he blushed.

We spoke at length about politics, art, and religion. Dr. Pettimore grew more and more exacerbated. We did not necessarily disagree on things but we damn sure didn't agree. He seemed not to have ever heard a point of view like mine on every topic that came up.

Clearly distressed, he said, "Well enough with the small talk. Let's get down to the brass tacks of our meeting today. I'd like for you to take few tests so that we can determine what classes to schedule for the coming school year."

"Yes, sir."

I took the first test in about half the time he thought it would take. It was a test with basic math problems, which I abhor, as well as reading comprehension and a smattering of history and non-mathematical problem-solving. I got up to go pee, and when I returned he was hunched over his desk looking at my answers. He looked up at me and shook his head.

"Roxanne, have you seen this test before?" he asked

"No, sir. Why?"

"I was just wondering. Sit down. I want you to take this test also."

"My God! This thing has three hundred questions Dr. Pettimore! We'll be here all day!"

"You got somewhere you need to be, young lady?" he said, raising his voice.

"No sir, but is this really necessary?" I replied slightly louder.

"Look. Do every other question. We'll break for lunch in an hour. Ok? Humor an old man."

I agreed and sat down. It was hot as all hell, and I made a point to unbutton my shirt a little more than usual. He tried his best not to be obvious about staring, and I pretended not to notice. I focused on the task at hand, and when I finished we went to lunch.

"Dr. Pettimore, if it's all the same to you, I'd just as soon not finish that test when we get back," I pleaded

"Why's that?"

"It bores me. It's of no interest to me at all. I'm not entirely sure what I want to do with my life but I'm fairly certain that being book smart isn't at the top of my list. Don't get me wrong, I think education is a noble endeavor, but I also think that education in what interests a soul is more relative."

"And just what does interest you, Roxanne?"

"I want to go places and see things. I want to meet people from all walks and learn from them. I want to be able to support myself and my kids doing things that I enjoy. I want to look back over my shoulder one day when I'm old and tired and feel like I got my money's worth out of the ride, and I'd like to think that somewhere along the way, I was a positive influence on somebody if only for a moment.

Most of all, I want everybody to quit asking me what I plan to do with my life!"

"Dangit Roxanne! Life just ain't that simple! Hell, I'd like to hop a freight train to Nashville and go to the Grand Ole Opry Saturday night Roxanne but it just ain't gonna happen!" he shouted.

"Dr. Pettimore, you're too damn fat to hop a train, but God knows you have enough money and time on your hands to hire a limousine to haul your ass to Nashville if that's what you want to do. The only thing stopping you is your own notion that it's somehow frivolous and irresponsible to do what your heart desires. I don't believe that! Not for one damn minute do I believe that and I never will," I countered.

He sat quietly considering not what I had said but what he himself had always believed to be true and he sighed. The angst appeared to have been quelled if only for a moment. He recounted to me how his father forbade him to go to Orange Beach with his classmates when they graduated from high school and the lecture he had received about being a productive and responsible member of the community. He told me of his friend who drowned in the Gulf of Mexico while on that trip and how he had always resented his father for not letting him go. "I knew he was a weak swimmer. He would've listened to me when the warning flags were posted at the beach. I could've saved him." More than resenting his father, Dr. Pettimore felt ashamed of himself.

"Maybe you could have saved him and maybe not, Dr. Pettimore. It doesn't much matter either way. What does matter is there's not one good damned reason you can't go to the Grand Ole Opry and now we both know it."

"Roxanne, what I'm trying to say is, though enviable, your ideas of a life well lived are lacking in a couple of very important ingredients that do not necessarily go hand-in-hand: free time and a lot of money. That being said, let me re-phrase my original question. Have you any ideas that will provide a means to the end you desire?"

He had me and we both knew it. I was poor, uneducated and had no real skills to speak of. "No, sir. I do not. I do, however, intend to make the most of the chance I've been given."

Dr. Pettimore smiled ever so slightly and nodded his head. "I envy you, Roxanne. I really do. I hope that I might be of some help to you one day. I'd like nothing better than to know that you were able to realize your dreams with some small measure of assistance or advice I might have had the opportunity to pass on."

Charlie arrived a short time afterward and they asked me to wait outside.

"Well, Richard?" Charlie inquired.

Dr. Pettimore fanned his flushed face with his handsome straw hat and shook his head. "I don't know that I've ever met another like her Charlie. That damn kid is smart as hell. She might be bull-headed and misguided, but she's nobody's fool. If she can get over being pissed off at the world she could certainly leave a mark. She can be quite charming really."

"What about school?" Charlie asked

"I wouldn't force it on her if I were you. She'd have no trouble passing the General Equivalency Exam. Hell, I'd bet the limit that she could pass the SAT with a little preparation. She's real clear that classroom education is of no interest to her though. She has a very high IQ, Charlie. She's smarter than you and I both," he noted.

"I don't care. We've made a deal. She's a minor and as long as she's under my roof, she's going to attend school," Charlie said.

"Then send her to Roebuck. She'd be nothing but trouble in public school. It sounds like she's made acquaintances already. That would help sweep the stones off the path for her. I'm quite sure that gaining admission won't be an issue," Dr. Pettimore suggested.

"Maybe. I'll think about it and talk to Cynthia," Charlie countered.

Small talk aside, we rode home in relative quiet. "Got any plans this week?" Charlie asked.

"Not really. I do want to go over to the Farm Co-Op one day though. I'd like to know a little about how pecans are harvested and sold. I thought it might be a way for me to make some money if you and I can come up with an arrangement," I said.

"It's a lot of work," Charlie said.

"I'd rather work than steal. I'd probably get caught stealing anyway."

"How about I drop you by there tomorrow morning when I go to work? I'll introduce you around," Charlie suggested

When we got back to the farm, Cynthia was outside sweeping the yard. We all sat around the pitcher of sun tea and talked about the coming school year. Charlie and Cynthia were obsessed with my attending school.

Charlie started the conversation. "Richard says he thinks you'd do well at Roebuck, Roxanne."

Cynthia squealed with excitement. "I think that's a wonderful idea!" She exclaimed. "Charlie and I both went to Roebuck back in the stone age," she cajoled. "Collette and Patti both go to Roebuck, and Rory just graduated."

"I'll take you over there tomorrow when I pick you up at the Feed and Seed," Charlie said.

"Feed & Seed?" Cynthia asked.

"Never mind, Momma," Charlie replied.

"By the way, Collette called. She said that she and Rory were going to be out later and might stop by," Cynthia informed me.

Collette and Rory showed up just as we were having supper. They made themselves at home in the kitchen. We finished the BL&T sandwiches, and Rory asked if I wanted to go get a milkshake with him and Collette. I agreed and we started out the door. Halfway down the steps, Cynthia called me back in.

"I'll be right back," I said.

"Here. You'll need some money," Cynthia said as she handed me ten dollars.

I felt a little embarrassed. Not for taking the money but for not realizing that I would need it. "I'll bring you back the change," I said. "I promise."

This all seemed so foreign to me. I was more accustomed to some half-drunk old man that wanted to put his hands on me handing me money. More often than not, it would be an uncle or one of my mother's *friends*. More often than not, I did what I had to do.

It was twilight as we drove slowly out the long gravel drive. The smell of honeysuckle was so thick you could nearly scrape if off of your tongue. Lightning bugs lit up the pasture and the sun, already set, had abandoned an orange and gray sky. So much had happened since that day at the gas station in Phoenix City. It was, at times, overwhelming, exciting, and a little unnerving. My mind wandered. This was all so different from what I had left behind. I was both happy and sad. The Portuguese called it *saudade*. I was haunted by the past and fearful that my dreams for the future might never be realized. I listened to the words of John Prine. *Just give me one thing that I can hold on to...To believe in this living is just a hard way to go.* I had never had much to hold onto. I smiled and thought to myself that just as surely as the sun paints the sky at twilight, letting go of a disconcerting belief system would point towards an awakening. The drive-in was full of families with kids, loud rednecks, old folks, a few familiar faces, and more. We took a seat with Patti and some others. Collette and I went to the counter to order. I stood staring at the menu board. A boy our age walked up. He wore a plaid shirt with the sleeves cut off. Sunburned and drunk, he reeked of cigarette smoke. Leaning towards me, he said, "Why don't you sit with us, Sweetie? You don't belong with them."

Collette giggled and it pissed him off. "Watch your mouth bitch," he said. She was about to pop her cork. I told her to go sit down.

"I've got this," I said. He smiled thinking that he had won some sort of prize and took my arm. I was determined not to make a scene. "Look, some other time. Ok?" I tried to pull my arm back but he tightened his grip. My determination and patience quickly diluted and I reached for the large metal napkin dispenser. I swung and planted it squarely on his head. He staggered backward, slipped, and landed abruptly on his butt.

"You whore!" he shouted.

He reached for my ankle, but a large Brogan boot on his forearm stopped his progress. The old man stared down at him. He reached to help him up and whispered. "She might be a 'hoe but she ain't yo' 'hoe. Now get the hell outta here." It was the old man I had met downtown when Cynthia and I went to get our hair cut. Visibly shaken, the boy disappeared.

"Buy you a milkshake old man?"

"It's past my bedtime but I'll see you around," he replied. As he walked away, the police pulled up. Before they could get out of their car, the old man walked over and leaned into the window and spoke with the officer. The police left and I returned to our table. Collette was jabbering ninety miles an hour when Rory asked what the altercation was about.

"My past," I replied somberly.

"Do you know Mr. Gentry?" one of our parties asked.

"The old man? No, not really. I mean, we met in town one day but I didn't know his name."

"Be careful Roxanne. It's said that Gentry killed a man once," Rory cautioned.

"The sonofabitch must've deserved it," I thought to myself.

We left the drive in and drove toward the seemingly endless "Party at the Pond." Someone had brought fireworks and the potheads were all oohing and aahing with every burst. Collette wandered off to find Patti who was busy trying to find her clothes that had mysteriously disappeared from where they previously hung to dry after she had been tossed into the pond.

"I'm gonna miss this," Rory sighed.

"Going somewhere, Pilgrim?" I chuckled.

"School will be starting soon."

"I thought you graduated."

"I was talking about college, goofball," Rory replied, looking a little perplexed.

"Who'd you piss off?" I laughed.

"Nobody. It's what we do," he explained

"Not me. I have neither the time nor the interest. Where are you going?" I asked, seemingly interested.

"Colorado Springs," he said. "The Air Force Academy. They have a good engineering program and offered me a football scholarship. I'll be in the service following graduation and *hopefully,* I'll learn to fly jets. Maybe I'll even work in Huntsville one day."

My mood darkened hearing Rory talk. I was taken aback that someone close to my age actually had their life mapped out like that, and I felt a little embarrassed that I had no plan of my own.

"Come on. Let's go for a swim," Rory smiled.

We walked down to the pond. Rory stripped down to his underwear and dove in. I followed suit. Watching the fireworks burst, I drifted on my back following the sound of Rory's splashing. I rolled over and caught a glimpse of him sitting on something a short distance away. There was a large assemblage of inner tubes that had been lashed together with rope. Random scraps of plywood served as a deck. Rory hefted me up onto the makeshift raft. We sat quietly drifting and caught our collective breath.

"There's nothing wrong with having a plan you know," Rory said, sounding a little defensive.

"I know. I didn't say anything," I snapped back. I realized that perhaps Rory's plan wasn't entirely his own. "Do me a favor before you go?" I asked.

"Depends."

"Teach me to drive?" I asked sheepishly.

"What? Little Miss Badass Roxanne can't drive? How the hell did you miss out on that?" he laughed.

"I don't know. I have the idea of it all. I've just never done it for myself." I laughed back.

"Well, we'll just have to rectify that. How about tomorrow?" he beamed.

"I've got plans in the morning but tomorrow afternoon would be good," I said.

"So be it." Rory smiled.

I stood up. "I've got a splinter in my butt!" I laughed and dove back into the water.

Chapter 4

Tom Gentry & The Pecan Grove

I found it a little peculiar that Charlie simply dropped me off at the co-op the following morning. I was almost certain he would go in and hover a bit before deciding that I was ok on my own. Nonetheless, I went in and looked about the place. It was part hardware store and part feed mill. A wooden and glass display cabinet full of Case knives occupied a space near the front counter. There were clothes and shoes that hinted of an agrarian purpose. Albeit small, there was an offering of firearms and ammunition as well. Stacks of different types of animal feed housed a large amount of the available floor space. There were sacks of seed stock and a large section of husbandry supplies. Just outside the rear of the building was where the farm implements and fencing supplies rested under an expansive pole shed. A separate repository housed a large quantity of hay. Mice skittered about the mill where grain was ground and mixed for feed. The numerous feral cats took stock of the escape routes used by the mice.

The purveyor had allowed Roxanne time to roam about before approaching her. "You must be Ms. Benefield," he said

"Yes," I replied.

"I'm Max Halpern. Charlie said you'd be stopping in. Anything I can help you with?"

"Well sir, I was thinking about a small scale pecan operation."

"That orchard at Charlie's place paid his way through law school," Max said.

"That's what I hear," I replied.

"Well, Tom Gentry knows as much about the ins and outs of the pecan business as anybody I suppose. He's probably the best person to talk to. Come along and I'll introduce you."

We walked out to the feed mill. The air was dusty and the mill rattled and groaned as the sacks filled and were then sewn shut by the mill operator. They waited for a break in the process and Max shouted over at the operator.

"Tom! Someone is here to see you," he shouted.

He turned and looked over his shoulder, "Shoulda knowed," he said.

I smiled. "Come on old man. I'll buy you a Coke."

"I take it you two know each other?" Max quizzed.

"Yeah. We know each other," Tom spoke.

The old man dusted himself off and approached her. "Well?" he questioned.

"Well, what?" I replied.

"Coke machine is up front," he said.

We got a drink from the machine and walked out the front door. There was a large ceiling fan that mostly just kept the flies stirred up. Two cane bottom chairs sat opposite each other on either side of a large crate that was home to a checkerboard.

"What's on your mind?" Tom started.

"Pecans," I replied.

"What about pecans?"

"How does one go about gathering them and selling them and is it worthwhile?"

"Depends on what you call worthwhile I s'pose. If it's a quick dollar you're lookin' fo' it ain't worthwhile. If you a sucka for hard work with the hope of making an honest dollar, yeah, it's worthwhile. Thais a fair amount of money laying on the ground over where you're staying at. You just gotta pick it up a little at the time."

"Well, how do I get started?" Roxanne asked.

"If you're gonna gather and sell somebody else's pecans, the first thing you have to do is come up with a working 'rangement that suits both parties. Right now, Bill Danbury is over there cuttin' hay. Tomorrow he'll rake it and let it dry. He'll bring over a wagon and a few local boys once it's ready and bale it. He'll take half and Charlie'll keep half. It's a working arrangement."

"So, I do all the work and Charlie keeps half the money when the pecans are sold?" Roxanne asked.

"Didn't say that. I said you have to both agree on a worthwhile 'rangement. Besides, dem nuts belong to him," Tom Gentry huffed.

"Let's say we come to an agreement. Then what do I do? Surely growers don't just pick the things up one at a time," I said.

"Well, dats one way to do it," he laughed. "Might die of old age afore you git enuff of 'em to make a pie though!" he laughed, amused by my naivety.

The old man lit an unfiltered cigarette and rocked back in his chair. "If I had a mind to gather dem pecans at the Hardwick's, here's what I'd do. First, I'd put a hay rake behind that old Farmall tractor he's got over there. I'd set it so it was barely scratchin' the ground and work circles out from each tree. That rake 'll scratch 'em up from the clover and leaf litter so they lay on top. Any nuts that don't pop up to the surface most likely been there awhile and ain't no good enny how. After that, you should be able to gather 'em up into piles with a garden rake. After that, you bag 'em up and do whatever you are of a mind to do with them. Sell 'em whole, have 'em shelled and sorted, make candy, or just sit there and eat 'em raw," he said.

"What would you do with them?" I asked.

"Afore I dun anything, I'd git a fair samplin' of what's there and have a buyer look at 'em. Lots of things can affect pecan prices. Size, moisture content, grade, and quality all have a hand in prices. Dem pecans out there always done good but no one has harvested them in quite some time. Hell, I ain't sold no pecans in seven years. I have no idea what thais worth. There's one thing for sho' though. All pecans are worth something to somebody. I tell you what. You git me a 15-pound sack of 'em and we'll see what thais worth."

We played a game of checkers and drank our drinks. We talked at some length about no particular thing before I asked, "Is it true what they say?"

"What do you think?" He replied.

"What was it like?"

"Don't go finding out for yo'self."

Charlie showed up as we were finishing our game.

"I'd like to play the winner," he said.

Mr. Gentry stood and shook Charlie's hand, "It's good to see you, Mr. Hardwick," he said.

"You two have a good visit, Tom?" Charlie asked

"Yessuh, we always do. I think dis young lady wants to try her hand at the pecan bidness if the two of you can reach a workin' 'greement," Mr. Gentry countered.

"I wondered what you were up to. We'll talk about it on the way back. Right now, it looks like Tom is fixing to teach you a lesson in checkers," Charlie said.

Sure enough, Mr. Gentry cleaned the board and Charlie took my seat at the checkers table. I went inside and wandered around while they played. I found myself near an open window where I could hear them talking out on the porch.

"You doing ok, Tom?" Charlie inquired.

"Yessuh. I reckon I am. I'm able to get up and work every day. My bills is paid and to my knowledge, I ain't hurt 'ary a soul lately."

Charlie nodded. "You know Roxanne, Tom?" Charlie asked.

"Mr. Hardwick, I wouldn't harm a hair on her head," Tom said defensively.

"I know that, Tom. Take it easy."

"We met in town one day and I bumped into her at the drive-in one night. That's all. She came in axkin' 'bout pecans and I told her what little I knowed about pecans and that's that, Mr. Hardwick. I swear," Tom said.

"I'd be indebted to you for any help you can give her Tom. Just don't try to do it for her. She wouldn't like that," Charlie outlined.

Tom stood and said, "You caint ever be indebted to me Mr. Hardwick. Not never."

They came in and Tom went back to work in the feed mill. Charlie talked with Max about the price of hay and soybeans for a few minutes and we left.

"You think we can come to a working agreement on the pecan orchard Charlie?" I asked "I'm not afraid to work. It's just an idea. You said that orchard paid your way through law school."

"What did you have in mind Roxanne?" Charlie asked straight-faced.

"I'm not sure. Mr. Gentry said it would be best to get a sampling and have them looked at first," I answered.

"Well, Tom would know if anybody did. You start there and we'll work out the details later," Charlie replied.

"Do you think I could get Mr. Danbury to make a pass through the pecan grove with the hay rake? Mr. Gentry said it'd make it easier to pick some up for a sampling," I asked.

"I'll drop you off at the hayfield, and you and Bill can work that out," Charlie replied.

The Hardwick property was broken up by stands of timber and open pasture. A handful of private dirt roads crisscrossed the property to provide access. Charlie turned down the dirt road that ran along the back side of the pond and stopped at the hay field. I saw a tractor in the distance. Charlie blew his horn, and the man operating the tractor waved.

"I'll walk back," I smiled.

"Suit yourself," Charlie replied.

I clambered over the fence. The barbed wire snagged the seat of my jeans and I fell to the ground. I jumped up and brushed myself off hoping that I hadn't been seen flopping around like some epileptic buffoon. I walked across the pasture towards the truck and trailer located at the end of the field under some overhanging hickory trees. I was soon overcome by every imaginable winged insect native to the South. They were all over me. I brushed and swatted at them in vain until I reached the truck and trailer. There was a water cooler on the tailgate of the truck. I helped myself to the water until the tractor made its way back. As it got closer, I took stock of the operator. In between glances back towards the hay mower, I noticed that he was about my age. His hair was hidden under a cap. His skin was tanned as leather and he glistened with sweat. He pulled up and switched the tractor off. He pulled his cap off and a shock of blonde hair fell to his shoulders. I'd seen him at the pond before. He wiped his face off with a rag and started for the water cooler.

"Something I can help you with?" he asked.

He'd hardly glanced at me. The veins in his arms bulged and his upper body was taut. I felt a fluid wave of desire that made my legs tremble.

"Are you Mr. Danbury?" I felt my skin turn cold in the afternoon sun as soon as I had said it. He was obviously NOT *Mr. Danbury*.

He finished his drink and turned to walk towards me. "I'm Mitchell Danbury," he said. "*Mr.* Danbury would be my dad."

I tried desperately to gather my wits. After what seemed like hours, I composed myself enough to utter my request about passing through the pecan grove with the hay rake.

"Well, this is a hay *mower,*" he explained. "I won't be using the *rake* until tomorrow."

I just stood there. I had never felt so *girlie* in my life. I felt the sweat on the tip of my nose but was afraid to reach up and wipe it off. I was abashed.

"Is tomorrow ok?" he asked.

"Huh? Yes. Tomorrow would be great," I managed.

"Ok then. Glad it suits your schedule," He smirked. "Need a lift up to the road?" he asked.

"No. I'll just cut through the pines over to the house," I countered.

"Are you planning to pick ticks out of your hair for the rest of the day?" he asked. "If not, you might want to stay out of the pine trees."

"Good idea. I'll just walk up to the road. I don't want to hold you up any longer," I said. I turned to walk towards the road and Mitchell whistled.

"I sure like those jeans," he said. "Did you pay extra for the hole in the seat?" he laughed.

I reached back and felt the hole the barbed wire had torn in my jeans. I was mortified. My ass AND my panties were showing. I waved back as I cantered towards the road. The sound of his laugh diminished but my arousal only grew. I showered and fell asleep under the breeze of the fan. I woke up when I heard the knocking on the door and Rory hollering "Hey! You ready?" I managed to get my shorts halfway on before he charged around the bookcases that served as the wall to the bedroom.

"Oops, sorry," he said.

I stood with my back to him and zipped my pants.

"It's ok. Come on in," I replied.

He sat on the bed as I rustled about looking for some shoes. I turned and saw Rory lying face down on my bed. He was wearing shorts and sneakers but no shirt. His hair was pulled back in a ponytail. Suddenly, the big brother figure I had previously cast of Rory was replaced by something more beguiling. "What in the world is going on with you Roxanne?" wafted through my mind. I felt like a ball of string that might come unwound. We pulled out of the driveway in Rory's jeep. "Before you can drive, you have to know a little about how a car operates," Rory began. He went on to explain the mechanics of the internal combustion engine and how its power was transferred to the wheels to make the car move. I was completely disinterested. I didn't even want to drive.

"Turn here," I said as we approached the old road that ran alongside the creek past the Hardwick's. Rory drove speechless until the road ended at the grove of elm trees near a sandy shoal in the creek. Only the tumbling water and insects would we hear. I assumed an aggressive posture astride his lap and leaned in to kiss him.

"I've never done this," Rory confessed. I climbed off of his lap and stepped out of the Jeep. I took the blanket from the rear of the Jeep and walked to the driver's side.

"Come on," I said reaching for his hand. Rory was timid at first and aghast at the physical sensation that was my body and he convulsed uncontrollably.

"I'm sorry," he kept muttering.

"Shhhh. Don't say anything," I insisted. "You've nothing to apologize about."

We spent the next few hours in each other's embrace. I thought of my cousin Henry and that afternoon that was his last on this earth and how grateful I was for the purity of the physicality we shared that day. I was grateful on this day that I could give of myself what had been given to me. As surely as I would learn to drive over the next few days, Rory found out what it was like to be the new toy on the playground before he would leave for Colorado Springs and the Air Force Academy.

Mitchell Danbury met me at the pecan grove the next day and made a pass beneath a few of the trees with the hay rake. It didn't take long to realize just how many pecans there were. I thanked him for his time and tried not to appear amorous but was fairly certain that he knew better. Rory came over and I drove us to the co-op. I found Tom Gentry while Rory roamed around looking at flannel shirts and shotguns and pocket knives.

"What's in the sack?" Tom smiled. I poured the nuts out on the ground beneath the pole shed. Tom picked up a handful and cracked them. Pulling the meat out and looking at the nuts, he took his hat off and wiped the sweat from his brow.

"You hand pick these?"

"No. I used a shovel and a rake."

"I mean, did you sort through 'em or just take 'em as they lay?"

"I just gathered them up. Why?"

"Just axkin' I've got to take a catch gate over to Blakely, Ga. tomorrow. Thays a wholesaler over there I always done business with. I'll take 'em with me and see what he says."

Cynthia took me to Roebuck Academy the following day to register for school. Magnolia trees lined the driveway that passed beneath the brick and wrought iron entryway. Over the gated entry, a bronze plaque read "COGITARE". The campus of Roebuck Academy was unlike any school I had ever seen. It was spread out over a large tract of land dotted by athletic fields and buildings that were detached from one another and looked to be ancient. The grounds resembled a meticulously manicured garden, and the buildings were covered with ivy.

Registration was a relatively painless process. Everything was more or less "pre-arranged" by Charlie and Dr. Pettimore. I met my counselor who helped me with class selections and then met briefly with Headmaster Harley Langston. Headmaster Langston married into the Roebuck family by way of the founder's great-granddaughter. His hair was disheveled. There was a subdued bouquet about him that pointed to cigarettes and vodka. He wore a noticeably mismatched pair of socks. I did my best not to laugh but doubted that he would notice if I did. Before leaving, we stopped at the commissary. Collette was there as was Patti and a handful of others. Everyone was trying on clothes but the clothes all looked alike.

"What in God's name are you wearing?" I asked Collette.

"The same thing you're fixing to be wearing," she laughed. "These are the school uniforms."

"Uniforms? I don't think so."

"See here young lady, you'll stir no pot of your foul brew here!" laughed Patti. "You just get in line with the rest of us!"

Cynthia explained that the wearing of uniforms was meant to put everyone on equal ground and to eliminate distraction from academic endeavors. Five pleated, gray plaid flannel skirts, five white shirts, five pairs of grey knee socks, and a pair of black and white saddle oxfords later, we returned to the farm. "What is Headmaster Langston's story?" I asked Cynthia.

She laughed out loud. "That is a very colorful story. He's actually very kind and very smart. Don't worry. You'll have little or no interaction with him," Cynthia replied.

"It's not me I'm worried about," I thought to myself.

Mitchell Danbury was finishing raking the hay fields when Cynthia and I returned to the house. Bill Danbury and

Charlie were having tea in the kitchen. Charlie introduced me to Mr. Danbury while Cynthia refilled their glasses.

"You ready for school to start young lady?" Mr. Danbury quizzed.

"Well sir, if I'm not, I suppose I will be when the day comes."

"We got uniforms today," Cynthia announced. "She looks so cute in them."

Charlie chuckled when I rolled my eyes. Bill Danbury cast a lascivious glance my way.

I excused myself and went to the loft in the barn to put away my clothes and to shower. The Danburys were gone when I came back down. The phone rang and Charlie answered it in the hallway that led from the kitchen to his study.

"Roxanne, it's for you. It's Tom Gentry."

I answered the phone and the old man said, "Git busy. You need to get dem pecans up and ready as soon as possible. Prices are good and there is a fair piece of money lying around out there just waiting for you to pick it up. Come by tomorrow and we'll talk."

He hung up without saying another word, and I walked back to the kitchen.

"What did Tom have to say?" Charlie asked.

"He said to get those pecans up and ready as soon as possible."

Rory gave me a ride to the store the following day. I found Tom bagging soybeans at the mill. I waited until he was finished sewing up the last bag of the order to greet him. I helped him load the 24 bags into the customer's pickup truck and we sat down to talk.

"What you have on the ground out there is last year's crop. Dem nuts have had nearly a year to dry which is good. The processor looks at moisture content as part of the price he's willing to pay. You'll need to get 'em up before this year's nuts start to drop though so you don't have a mixed bag. They don't like that. Now pecans in the shell are bringing thirty- nine cents a pound. That's not written in blood and this is a sort of odd time of year to sell pecans but never mind that. In the shell is the quickest and easiest way to sell 'em. Just gather 'em up and git 'em over to Blakely. They are worth more if they are shelled and picked clean but you ain't got what it takes for that. But you can get mo' money for nuts that are still in the shell but cracked. It makes it easier for the processor to shell 'em out. It's pretty simple if you know someone with a mechanical cracker that's willin' to hep out," Tom smiled and winked. Now you gonna have expenses. There's no gittin 'round that. First, there's Mr. Hardwick's cut. Thais his nuts. You'll need to have 'em cracked if you decide to go that route. Me and you kin work that out. You'll need to have 'em bagged up here at the mill and you'll have to get them over to Blakely. You'll need help getting them all up off the ground too. You ready to go to work?"

"Thirty-nine cents isn't much money," I sighed.

"You listen to me young lady," Tom scoffed. "You get thirty-nine cents out of your purty little head and think more along the lines of how you gonna make the most of what you've been given. If you think for one damn minute that thais a easier way to make money, you just think about the last hand of cards you played at the Palomino Club! Do you hear me?" I'm telling you thais a fair amount of money laying on the ground out there at the Hardwick place and it'll get you a far piece down the road if gettin' outta here is what you want. I can't say I'd blame you for that ennyway."

"Well, you don't have to get all pissy about it," I pleaded.

"You ain't seen me pissy and you don't want to," he said assuredly.

"What's the premium for cracked nuts?" I asked.

"I ain't gonna say 'cause I ain't sure. You'll have to dicker that when you get to Blakely."

"What about Charlie's share?"

"Offer him 10% after expenses. He'll huff and puff a little but stand your ground. I think he'll be reasonable enuff."

"You really think there's a lot of money lying on the ground out there?"

"Oh yeah, I know thay is. A helluva lot more than any poker hand you ever played," Tom grinned.

"Let's take a look at that mechanical cracker Old Man."

We walked out to the equipment shed where Tom pulled an old canvas tarp off of the cracker. It looked like a meat grinder run by a lawnmower motor that was bolted to a wooden bench.

"It might not look like much but it'll crack 50 pounds/hour easily. So long as you keep feedin' 'em to the hopper and don't run out of gas or break a belt."

Tom went on to show how the hopper attached to the cracker and how the cracked nuts dropped through the opening in the tabletop to the shelf below which would hold a large wash tub to collect the nuts.

"We'll need to replace the belt and attach it to the pulley and make sure she's all lined up and doesn't wobble.

An air cleaner and a new spark plug and it should be good to go."

I started to get excited. "This is real. This can work," I thought to myself. "You're a good man Tom Gentry. I thank you." I hugged the old man's neck and went to find Rory wandering around the store.

Rory dropped me off and left to go who knows where and with who knows who. I ran in and found Charlie in his study. "You got a minute?"

"Yes, ma'am. What's on your mind?"

"Pecans. I met with Tom and he went over everything with me. I feel like it's an opportunity I'd like to take advantage of. I understand it's a lot of work and not something I'd get rich doing. With the exception of your cut, I have a fair idea of the costs. I'd like to offer you 4% of the market price for in-shell nuts. Tom Gentry will verify the weight when I have them bagged at the mill. At 4% I feel like it would be a worthwhile endeavor."

Charlie was sipping a tumbler of whiskey when I made my offer. He got whiskey in his nose when he started to choke. After thrashing about the study and turning a bright red he caught his breath.

"Good God almighty child! Worthwhile? I'd say so. Hellfire and damnation, we used to have hordes of people begging to pick those nuts on halves for years!" 50-50 was always a worthwhile endeavor for both parties. I don't see why it wouldn't be now."

"When was the last time somebody came through here and offered you something like that? Times have changed Charlie. Mechanical equipment and commercial leasing operations have made that sort of arrangement a thing of the past for someone with a small grove like yours. Nobody will bother with a grove that small. Besides, 4% is more than you get for letting those nuts just lie on the ground out there year after year."

"Tom Gentry put you up to this?"

"No Sir. Absolutely not."

"I'll consider your offer. I won't consider it very seriously, but I'll consider it."

"There's one other thing, Charlie. I'll need for you to hook a hay rake up to that old Farmall tractor and rake 'em up where I can gather them for bagging."

Charlie just shook his head and went back to reading his University of Alabama Law Review. I went up to the barn loft and read for a while before falling asleep. I dreamed of neon lights and large crowds of people laughing and of children crying. I saw a highway with no end that pierced a stark landscape of sparse vegetation and odd rock formations. A high dessert meadow held a herd of bison below the slopes that were covered in aspen trees that had turned golden in the autumnal months. I awoke in the twilight and lay quiet and listened to the sounds of the receding day. The sounds of the katydid and cicada muted the yelping of the coyotes to a whimper. I listened to the owls that carried out their mournful conversation from opposing locales. I thought of Santiago in Hemingway's Old Man and the Sea and of his determination that would not be denied despite circumstances that might dictate otherwise. "What will be my lions on the beach?" I wondered. I heard a car coming down the long dirt and gravel driveway from the road, and the loft gathered in the headlights that had been turned on. Charlie and Cynthia I thought to myself. I stepped out on the landing. It was Mitchell Danbury.

"Aw hell," I thought to myself. "You're done now."

"You forget something?" I called out.

"No, not exactly. I thought I'd see if you wanted to go watch the star shower."

My legs trembled and my skin felt cold. "Star shower? Is that the best you can come up with?"

Mitchell walked halfway up the steps. He got just close enough to where we could actually see each other's eyes.

"I'm not sure what you think of me or what you might have heard about me but I ain't the Boogie Man. I won't chop you up and throw you in the river. Put on some bug spray and grab a blanket. I'll bring you home whenever you say."

"Wait here," I replied. I went in and grabbed a bag and a blanket. We pulled out of the driveway and onto the road. Mitchell dialed the radio to a country station.

"Where we headed?" I asked.

"Not far. Over to the hayfield should be a good spot. Away from that light pole back there."

Mitchell stopped and I opened the gate that led to the hayfield. I shut the gate after he drove through and closed the latch. The headlights caught the attention of a group of grazing deer. Their eyes glowed in the light until Mitchell turned them off. When he turned the lights back on, the deer were gone. We drove a short distance into the field before stopping. "Why don't you pick out some music?" Mitchell said as he got out. I dug through the box full of tapes and selected Pink Floyd and put it in the tape deck. Mitchell had opened the sliding rear window in the cab of the truck and was clamoring around outside. "Good choice," he said. He was busy inflating an air mattress with a foot pump.

"Now, what is that supposed to be for?"

"It's to lay on and watch the star shower," he replied.

"Who the hell said anything about laying down?"

"Well, I tell you what. You just stand there flat footed and stare up at the sky and let me know how that works out for you. I'm gonna lay down."

I started to argue and Mitchell picked me up at the waist and sat me on the tailgate of the truck as effortlessly as I had seen him loading finished hay bales. "Why don't you just sit right here and roll us a smoke. If I wanted to get in your pants I'd just come right out and say so."

Mitchell handed me a baggie and a pack of TOP rolling papers. He continued pumping up the mattress while I rolled a joint by the light of the cargo light on the cab of the truck. I sprayed some bug spray to ward off the mosquitos and hopped down off the tailgate.

"Give me a hand with this mattress please," he said.

We lifted it up into the bed of the truck and sat on the tailgate. Mitchell lit the joint and drew heavily on it before passing it to me. He hopped down and went back to the cab of the truck.

"Do you ever sit still?" I asked. Mitchell didn't reply. He turned the music up and came back to the tailgate with a cold bottle of Ripple wine.

"Well, you just thought of everything. Didn't you? You treat all the girls this special?"

"No. Just the ones with red hair," he laughed.

The wine and the weed predictably eased my weakened inhibitions to the point that the inevitable consummation transpired. Afterward, we lay quietly and watched as the meteors streaked through the darkness. It really was quite beautiful and I thought of what Tom Gentry had told me the first time we met. I was satiated. I was also pleased when he asked about the pecans.

"I'll need some help for sure. That hay rake did the trick. Probably wouldn't take terribly long to go through the whole grove," I put forth. "You available? I could probably furnish the equipment if you'd operate it."

"Maybe. I'd need to do it pretty soon though."

"I'll know more tomorrow," I explained. "I won't keep you hanging. Thank you."

We drove back to the house around 11 pm. I recalled that Cynthia and Charlie were out playing bridge. That explained their absence. I felt some relief not having to explain my whereabouts while I was still a bit foggy. It just made things simpler I thought to myself.

"Why don't you come over tomorrow evening? Charlie and his golfing buddies and their wives all come over on Saturday and cookout."

"I don't know. I don't exactly run with that crowd if you know what I mean."

"It's not like you think," I replied. "Think about it."

Knowing that Charlie would be up early, I too rose and went down to the house the following morning.

"You're up early," Cynthia noted.

"I was hoping to catch Charlie before he heads out."

"If it's about your proposal on the pecans, I wouldn't get my hopes up. He was a little miffed at your offer."

"Did you smooth him over for me?" I asked

"I think so," Cynthia replied.

We both snickered but changed the subject to cooking out that night when we heard Charlie walking down the stairs.

"Well if it isn't the Pecan Queen! Have you given any further thought to a realistic arrangement for the pecan grove Roxanne?"

"No, sir. I wanted to see what you had to say."

"What I have to say is no. I'm not unreasonable though. I'll consider 10% of the in-shell price. You're on your own as far as gathering them up and getting them to market though. I was born at night but it wasn't last night. There's one other thing as well. I'll need you to work with me at the courthouse two or three days a week after school."

"Well is it two or is it three and for how long?"

Cynthia choked trying to hide her snicker and milk ran out of her nose.

"Damnit, woman! Don't encourage this behavior! Two days a week for as long as you are here."

We ate quietly for a minute. Talk soon turned to who was coming over and what we'd be cooking on the grill that night.

"Mitchell Danbury might come over if that's alright."

Their faces took on a rather pensive appearance.

"What?" I reflected.

"Nothing. We like Mitchell. He's always welcome here," Cynthia said.

"Mitchell is quite a bit older than you Roxanne," Charlie said.

"Don't worry. I don't think he'll chop me up and throw me in the river or anything," I mused.

After breakfast, I followed Charlie out as he got his golf clubs and shoes ready to go to the club for the day.

"I'll go 7% in shell Charlie. I'll work for you three days a week instead of two but I want my work to suffice in covering my room and board. I'll handle the labor if you'll let me borrow your equipment including that stake body truck to take the nuts to Blakely."

"You pay for the gas and oil. Caddy for me one Saturday a month at the club. That's the end of my rope."

"Done!" I said. and we shook hands.

I called Mitchell later that morning and asked him to come over. I watched as he got Charlie's tractor and hay rake hooked up and we set out for the pecan grove. It didn't take long for me to realize two things that were a certainty. There were a lot of pecans in that little grove and gathering them was not going to be a walk in the park. Fortunately, the grove was relatively free of litter and the nuts were, for the most part, clean. It wasn't long before Mitchell was finished.

"There you are. That's about all a hay rake and a Farmall tractor can do for a big time nut harvester," Mitchell observed.

Rory drove up.

"I'll get the tractor back," Mitchell said.

"You coming over later?" I asked

"I don't know. Maybe. We'll see."

In passing, Mitchell and Rory exchanged pleasantries.

"Wow. You're really going to do it huh?"

I nodded and shrugged my shoulders.

"It's a little overwhelming," I observed.

"You just have to break it up into small chunks. If you look at it all at one time it's overwhelming. Pick you out a 10x10 patch of ground and it's not so difficult."

"I suppose. Can you run me to the co-op? I want to get some bags at the feed mill."

"Sure. Let's go. You drive."

Mr. Halpern agreed to let me have the bags and a pair of gloves on credit and we left.

"You coming over later?" I asked of Rory.

"Yeah. I've got a hot date too," He smiled.

For some odd reason, I felt both slighted and proud.

"You go get 'em," I smiled.

"Roxanne, I'll always love you," Rory said in a near apologetic tone.

I smiled and he left after we dropped the bags off at the pecan grove. I went straight to work raking pecans and shoveling them into the nylon sacks. Within a few hours, I had amassed quite a few bags of nuts that were nearly too heavy to move. My pulse quickened and I grew excited at the prospect. I worked until Cynthia showed up.

"You gonna help me with the cookout?"

"What time is it?" I inquired.

"Past 4 o'clock. Charlie and his crew will be home before long."

"Damn. I lost track of time. I'll be right there."

I finished the bag I was working on and hurried back to the house. I peeled potatoes for the potato salad while Cynthia shucked corn. I brought in the three one gallon glass containers full of sun brewed tea and patted out some hamburgers for the grill. The regular attendees started to trickle in and I excused myself to go and take a bath. Before I could get the soap out of my hair, Collette and Patti came running up the steps. They stormed through the door and presented themselves on my side of the dressing screens that acted as walls for the bathroom.

"Oh my God! Mitchell Danbury?" they squealed in unison.

"What in the world are you talking about?"

"He's down at the house. Cynthia and Charlie have him under a bright light for the inquisition."

"Damnit!" I panicked.

I finished rinsing my hair and jumped naked out of the tub and grabbed a towel.

"It's alright. We rescued him. He's on his way up here."

"What? I'm butt ass naked Collette! Go stop him, please. I'll be out in a minute."

"You mean to tell me he hasn't seen you naked, Roxanne? I know you and Mitchell Danbury both better than that," Collette laughed.

"You don't know diddly squat Collette. There's nothing *to* know. Maybe you can tell us how you know him so well," I replied. "And what are you giggling about Miss I Can't Find My Panties?" I pointed at Patti.

The three of us looked at each other and laughed hysterically. When we walked into the sitting area and saw Mitchell sitting there with the guitar, we all wondered how long he'd been there and what he had or had not heard.

"I've heard rumors of this guitar but never believed it really existed," He said. "Needs some strings and a little TLC."

"Well, Collette? You and Patti want to go see if dinner is ready?"

Patti took Collette by the arm before she could speak and they walked down the stairs towards the house. As soon as they were halfway down the stairs, Mitchell and I both started to speak at the same time. I held up my hand. "Look, I like you. That is to say, I like what little I know of you. You've been a big help with the pecans and last night was great, but I'm not one to be tied down and I'm not one to hold someone else's hands behind their back and make them walk a straight line either. Most of all, I don't think the whole county needs to know any details regarding what we might or might not be doing after dark. I'm not ashamed in the least of sharing myself with you, but I'll be damned if you'll make a fool of me for doing so by telling all of you friends. If you can walk the same path, good. If not, we can part ways now. There's one last thing. You can't just walk in here unannounced."

Mitchell sat quietly nodding his head and stared at me for a few minutes. I felt a bead of sweat roll down my rib cage.

"You're a beautiful woman Roxanne Benefield. Now if you don't mind, I'm a little hungry. Let's go flip some burgers."

My face was fully flushed. No one had ever referred to me as a woman, much less a beautiful woman. We went down to the house. Charlie and his friends were pitching horseshoes and the women were having cocktails. Mitchell went to throw horseshoes and I checked the grill and went into the kitchen. Patti and Collette were slicing onions and cheese and getting condiments ready. Both of them had been in the blender full of daiquiris and were getting a little goofy. They talked about the coming school year. I spoke of pecans and making enough money to leave when school was out.

"Where exactly will you go first, Roxanne? Certainly, you've given some thought to it," I heard someone ask.

It was Cynthia and Collette's mom.

"Biloxi. I'd like to spend some time near the ocean. Then I'd like to go to New Orleans. I've read quite a bit about the culture and history there. I plan to see the state of Texas from Houston to El Paso then travel along the Continental Divide to Wyoming then west towards Salt Lake City, Las Vegas, then to the Pacific Ocean. I've never seen a landscape that consisted of more than pine trees and kudzu and the most exotic creature I've ever seen is a whitetail deer."

"What about Mitchell? He's exotic," snickered Patti. The others all started to howl and spill their drinks.

"No, he's just wild. There's a difference," I laughed.

We finished in the kitchen and went outside to cook. Mitchell and I took turns flipping hamburgers and pitching horseshoes. I was busy soundly whipping them all at horseshoes when dinner was ready. "Come get 'em," Mitchell announced.

We all circled around the grill and condiments. We drank tea and Cokes for the time being. Mitchell and Rory seemed to have found some sort of common ground and were seemingly enjoying each other's company. I was so proud to have both of them in my life if just for a moment. Suddenly, I felt as though I was not a part of the current landscape but rather an observer of its characters. Patti and Collette looked exactly like their mothers. As surely as Collette's dad was sincere in his interest of everything Dr. Pettimore had to say about the coming football season; Rory was similarly interested in hearing of Mitchell's plans for working the offshore oil fields in Louisiana. Cynthia and Charlie, on the other hand, seemed somewhat disengaged. They were loved and respected by all but when Jessica died, a part of them died as well. I became acutely aware of all I had lost. Henry, my grandparents, Travis, Mac, and my innocence were all gone. I had never lived as a child. I felt the back of my neck turn cold as I began to sweat profusely. I slipped quietly inside to the bathroom where I fainted. I lay on the cold tile floor for a minute, and then I got up and wiped my face with a cold, wet washcloth as I stared into the mirror. I wanted to run. I had wanted to run for as long as I could remember.

I worked feverishly those last few weeks before school started. When I wasn't in the grove bagging pecans, I was at the co-op running the nutcracker. Tom Gentry would remove them from the litter screen and bag them up so I could keep feeding the whole nuts into the hopper. We talked at great lengths about many things. He spoke of his childhood and the struggles of the Great Depression and of the horrors of war. He talked at length of the things he had only hinted of the day we first met. I mostly just listened. I suspected I was the only person he had ever recounted his experiences to and I wondered why.

Friends would stop by occasionally to help out in the grove. Even Charlie and Cynthia pitched in once in a while. Mitchell helped when he wasn't working for his dad. We found out that by re-raking the grove with the hay rake set at an angle, the nuts fell into neat rows making them easier to gather. I'd get up early before the sun grew hot and work until late morning. I'd shower and drop nuts off at the co-op before going to Charlie's office at the courthouse so I could fulfill my obligations there. I'd work with Charlie until 3 or 4 o'clock and then either crack nuts or return to the grove to pick more up. Tom Gentry kept up with the weights for me and stored the nuts at the feed mill. It was one day at the co-op that Tom Gentry pointed out that I had more nuts than he could store and that it was time to make a trip to Blakely.

"Can I ask a favor, Tom?"

"Ain't no harm in axkin'."

"Go with me. I can speak for myself. I just want you to come with me."

"Why?"

"I don't want to know how much money there is until it's all said and done. I'm afraid I'll get excited and quit where I am or get disappointed and give up. I want you to handle the money. Pay my debts and give me what's left when it's all settled. Will you do that for me?"

"Miss Roxanne, I don't mind heppin' enny way I kin, but folks might not think too highly of you taking off across the state line with the likes of me."

"You surely have me confused with someone that gives a damn what other people think Tom Gentry. I'll let Charlie know and that's all that matters."

Charlie had excused my caddy duties at the club with my offer to serve three days instead of two at the DA's office. This left Saturday open for Tom and me to drive to Blakely. We loaded the stake body truck at the feed mill before the co-op opened that morning. We checked the tires and oil, and we filled the gas tank at the service station where Charlie had set up an account for me to buy gas. Gentry nodded in the passenger's seat while I drove.

Tom Gentry introduced me to the proprietor when we arrived. "Let's get those nuts unloaded and weighed young lady. I'll cut you a check and y'all can be on your way."

Tom had already started pulling some of the bags off of the truck when I stopped him.

"Seems to me that maybe we should agree on a price first."

"Well, I've seen what you have Little Missy and thirty-nine cents is what I told ol' Tom here," the proprietor cajoled, his arm around Tom's shoulder.

"My name is Roxanne. Thirty-nine cents is certainly a fair price for in-shell nuts sir, but I've brought these nuts cracked, screened and bagged."

"You shouldn't have wasted your time. Cracked nuts mean little or nothing special to me. We can open those bags and empty them and you can take the bags back with you. I have no need for them."

I had done some snooping around and made some phone calls from Charlie's office to the University of Georgia Experiment Station in Tifton, Ga. My sources had informed me that pecan warehouse stores were marginal as compared to demand and that the prospect for the next crop was less than desirable. Pecan trees, as it turned out, bear heavily one year and very little the next. I was sitting in the catbird's seat as Granny would say.

"Now you and I both know that cracked nuts bring a premium, and we both know why. Let's not pull each other's chain. I'll take forty-seven cents per pound, and I'll bring the rest of them when they're ready."

Tom Gentry was aghast but stood silently there on the dock at the warehouse.

"Great God Almighty! Is one of those bags full of gold or are you just full of crap?"

"You play cards, mister?" I asked.

"What in the name of Sam Hill are you talking about?"

"I'll bet the house that if we take a walk through your warehouse it's damn near empty. You ain't got squat for the holiday season, and you need all you can get."

"Look here, Missy. You might think you're farting through silk but I wouldn't give you forty-seven cents a pound for those nuts if they were the last ones to be had!" he squawked.

"You're no fool mister. I can see that. Neither am I. I've done my homework and I'm sure you have as well. The coming crop of pecans is going to be poor. You know that and I know that. I also know there is a fair amount of scab being reported. These nuts are clean. They are dry and they will bring a premium price."

I could tell by the look on his face that he was about to fold his hand. I stood quietly and stared. I knew that the next one to speak would pay the price for doing so.

"Wait right here," he said and walked inside.

"I'll go forty-three cents seeing that they are cracked," he said.

I turned to Tom. "You got time to go to Albany, Tom?"

"Damnit, woman! I'll do forty-five cents and you'll not get that in Albany or anyplace else!" he demanded.

"Cash, no checks," I demanded.

"Done," he said.

I had brought along a fifty-pound sack of fertilizer from the co-op with us. I pulled it off and laid it on the scales to verify their accuracy and then set it aside.

The mood got much lighter as he and Tom unloaded the bags and carefully recorded their weights.

"Come on in," he invited.

"Tom, I'll wait here. You go on in with this gentleman."

We shook hands. "I'll get the rest of them here as soon as I can," I said.

"I'll be right here, ma'am." He smiled.

We had just gotten onto the highway when I noticed the grin on Tom Gentry's face.

"What?" I asked.

"You one bad white girl Miss Roxanne! I swear I ain't ever knowed a woman quite like you! You wrapped that man up and spanked his bottom like you'd done that a thousand times befo'!"

"I just did a little homework, Tom. That's all."

"Uh huh. Well, it looked like a ass-whoopin' to me!" He said slapping his knee. "You know how much money I got here Miss Roxanne?"

"No. I told you I don't want to know either. Not until it's all over."

"A ass-whoopin'. That's what that was." He must've said it a dozen times on the way back.

When I dropped Tom off at the Circle City Feed and Seed he tried to hand me the envelope that contained the money from the pecans.

"Tom, you agreed to take care of this. Don't hand me the money until it's all said and done. I want you to go inside and settle my debt with Mr. Halpern. I need another pair of gloves and some more bags. Go ahead and pay for those. I'm going to fill the truck up with gas. When you leave here, pay my bill at the service station as well."

"Yes, ma'am," he replied. As I started the engine, Tom extended his hand to me. We shook hands and I turned on the radio.

"Roxanne? Iffin' you don't know how much money thais in here, how you gonna know if ever'thang is what it should be when the dust settles?" Tom asked while scratching his head.

"You kept a running list of the number of pounds of shelled nuts we weighed in Blakely in that little notepad. Right? I already know the scales in Blakely were right. We checked them. Remember? I know the price per pound we agreed on. Write down how much you pay out for my debts. We have a record of the in-shell weights out there in the shed by the cracker. I'll use that to pay Mr. Hardwick. It'll be fine Tom."

Once there were enough pecans for another load, Tom and I made another trip to Blakely and met with the wholesaler. Time was moving quickly against my goal of being finished before the start of school. More than once was the evening I would work by the headlights of the old truck in my effort to finish. My legs and back were constantly tired. I had resorted to wearing knee pads so that I could occasionally rest my back and legs by crawling about the grove. My hands ached but it seemed a damn sight better than working the killing floor of a chicken plant I thought to myself.

My "by invitation only" policy with Mitchell had not lasted very long. He would climb the stairwell to the loft and let himself in but not before checking in with the Hardwicks to let them know he was there. Once inside he'd sit and play that old guitar while I bathed. Later, he would massage my back and legs with lotion. My favorite, however, was the hand massage. One hand at a time, he would start by rubbing my palm before moving to the heel pad and then the thumb pad. Mitchell would firmly grip each finger and squeeze lightly. He would then pull each finger gently until there was a pop. Finally, with his fingertips against mine, he would gently push, stretching all of the muscles, ligaments and tendons in the hand and wrist and then release. Sometimes we went out. Most of the time we stayed in.

There would not be enough time to crack the remaining nuts, and they would have to be sold in-shell. I had an idea to offset the reduced earnings and kept some of the nuts for myself at the equipment shed to shell out as time permitted. I put in a call for help at the pond one night and finishing the harvest was put to rest in short order. The last of the nuts were bagged and their weights recorded on Tom Gentry's clipboard at the feed mill, and we made our final trip to Blakely. Having concluded our business in Blakely, I had Tom finish paying my debts to Mr. Halpern for supplies and the service station for gas and oil.

All that remained was settling with Charlie. I reported for work at the courthouse the following day. Most of my tasks at the District Attorney's office were rudimentary. Filing, delivering court documents between offices and answering the phone filled most of my afternoons. I sat down in Charlie's office near the end of the day as he finished pouring over the court docket.

"Something I can do for you?" he asked

"Yes, sir. I'd like to go over our settlement when you're finished."

Charlie returned to his court docket and handed me a deposition to take to the Sheriff's office.

"I'll be done when you get back," Charlie said.

I had handwritten a ledger that accounted for all matters regarding the pecans. Supporting documents in hand and arithmetic double checked, I showed Charlie the in shell weights Tom recorded at the mill and a receipt from the wholesaler in Blakely showing .39/lb. for the in-shell nuts I had taken him and the resulting dollar amount that I owed Charlie.

"This receipt from the wholesaler," he began. "The weight is nowhere near the total that you show here," He continued.

"I sold most of the pecans cracked at a higher price. Our agreement was 7% of the in-shell price," I said as I slid the envelope of cash across the desk.

Charlie smiled and reared back in his chair. "Well, that explains why you haven't been home much. Cynthia sent me out one evening around supper time to get you. I went to the pecan grove and watched you for a while. I wasn't sure what I felt when I saw you down on your knees bagging those damned pecans. I wasn't sure if I felt sorry for you or if I was proud of you or if I was envious. The one thing I was sure of was that you were going to be alright and that makes me very happy."

Charlie picked up the envelope. "Let's go home," he said.

Chapter 5

Dove Shoot

School was scheduled to start the day after Labor Day. The Saturday prior marked the opening day of dove hunting. There would be no golf at the club and no cookout at the Hardwick's. As tradition would have it, Max Halpern would host a dove shoot and barbecue at his place. Each spring, Max planted a large field of sunflowers. At one end of the field was a stand of hardwoods, and at the other, a small pond. By late summer, Max had decided that the sunflowers were of no use and had not produced enough to warrant harvesting. Instead, he mowed them down with a bush hog. By design, this drove the migratory birds into a feeding frenzy. The landscape offered a safe place for the birds to roost in the hardwoods and a water source at the other end of the field. In between lay an all you could eat buffet of sunflower seeds. Some called it shooting over a baited field. Others called it responsible land management. Since every politician, law enforcement officer and game warden in three counties attended, there was no further discussion regarding the matter.

Hunters paid a fee to offset the costs of the event and were assigned shooting stations in sets of two to six shooters. Hay bales were strategically arranged to provide cover for the hunters and to offer seating and storage for guns and shotgun shells as well as coolers with ice and beverages. At their discretion, hunters were permitted to have an attendant to assist with retrieving fallen birds, pouring beverages, and lending advice and encouragement. I jumped at the opportunity when Max Halpern said that he could use some help in his blind.

"The job pays $10 per shooter plus tips for the day. I have four shooters in my blind. We have a standing bet of $100 with Bill Danbury's group each year. There is also a $200 payout to the overall winner. The most important thing you can do is make sure you pick up every bird that hits the ground. I hate losing, and we've lost the bet with Bill Danbury the past four years in a row. It'll be hectic in the morning and again in the evening. The middle part of the day is largely a lot of tall tales and business talk. I think you'll do well."

I met Max Friday afternoon to load supplies onto his truck. There were folding chairs, a small card table, a large cooler with ice, several smaller coolers, soft drinks, snacks and a case of shotgun shells. We went to his farm and rode out to the blind to unload supplies for the hunt. After setting up, we rode back to his house.

Max Halpern's farm was not a hobby farm but a working farm. He had a sizable cattle operation, and he also grew corn and soybeans. His son Matthew and his wife had a house on the property. Matthew saw to most of the farm business while Max ran the Circle City Feed and Seed operation. Max's wife Charlotte did the bookkeeping for both operations. I recognized Tom Gentry's old truck parked near a pole barn some distance from the main house. I saw the glow of a fire and a wisp of smoke that smelled of green hickory.

"Max Halpern! We have a million things to go over," Charlotte pleaded.

"Why don't you go check on Tom?" This won't take long," Max assured me.

"Take your time."

I stopped short of the entrance to the barn when I heard singing. The voice was despondent. It was Hank Williams' Cold, Cold Heart. I had heard it on the radio years before and was haunted by the lyrics. I peeked through the door and saw Mitchell sitting in a circle with Tom Gentry and a couple of others. Mitchell was singing. When he finished, the men spoke and passed around a bottle of apple brandy. Tom Gentry played next. I was mesmerized. I dared not enter the building. It somehow seemed invasive. Tom played Come On In My Kitchen on slide guitar. There was an old man to his left that played the harp. Tom sang another song that was, from what I could gather, about the love between a man and a woman that had betrayed him. I had never heard anything quite like it. I watched and listened until I heard the screen door shut at the main house. I turned and walked back to meet Mr. Halpern.

"Come on. I'll get you back to Charlie's place," he said.

The morning portion of the shoot the following day was as Max Halpern had described it would be. Birds flew in great numbers between the stand of hardwood trees and the small pond that provided water as they surveyed the ground below. It was all I could do to keep up. Between marking downed birds for retrieval and making sure everyone was comfortable and had what they needed, there was little time left for socializing. There was one member of the party in the blind that was having a considerable amount of trouble knocking any birds out of the air above the field. I watched for a moment before I approached him.

"Can I suggest something?"

"Hell! It couldn't hurt. This is embarrassing."

"I'm no expert, but I've noticed something. When you swing your shotgun toward your target, you stop as soon as you pull the trigger."

"Yeah?"

"Well, the bird keeps flying. It seems to me that if you continue to swing *past* the bird as you pull the trigger they'll run right into it."

"I'm shooting behind them? Is that what you're saying?" he asked.

"Yeah, I think so."

Soon afterward, he was dropping birds at a frantic pace. Everyone else just kind of watched. Each report of his gun was followed by a cloud of feathers and a bird helicoptering towards the ground. We broke for BBQ around mid-day when the flight slowed. It was hot and I was tired but Max insisted I join in the festivities. There were other women there. Wives mostly but I did see Patti who was working the blind that Rory was in. A few other girls from the Party at the Pond were there as well. We ate BBQ and visited until it was time to go back to the blind. When I got back to our assigned shooting station, I was approached by one of the shooters in our party.

"Can you watch me shoot? Maybe give me some pointers?" he asked shyly.

"Sure. I'll try," I promised.

He was young and quiet. A little bashful, he blushed. When the hunt resumed, I made sure everyone had shotgun shells and drinks, and then I watched the boy shoot. I walked over and asked if he ever played football. He said that he had always played and that he was pretty good. I reminded him that a good quarterback throws the ball not where the receiver is but where he's going to be.

"Watch the flight line of the bird. Pick out a point ahead of its flight and shoot," I told him.

He shot three in succession and blushed with pride when I brought them back to the blind. When the shooting ended that afternoon, everyone returned to the main house and tallied the harvest. Our blind had won the overall payout *and* the side bet with Bill Danbury's group. There was a great deal of celebration and congratulations as the day wound down.

"You sure you weren't picking up somebody else's birds, Max?" Bill Danbury joked.

"I'm sure, but we did have a ringer on our side," he chided and put his arm around my shoulder.

"You are something else, Roxanne," Max said. "I'm proud to know you and want you to know if there's anything I can ever do for you just let me know."

He handed me an envelope. It was my $40 plus an equal share of the overall prize and the side bet with Bill Danbury. I thanked him and the other members of our group.

Judge Thompson, who I had previously appeared before in court, came up to me and said, "Young lady, in my line of work I have to be objective in order to be fair. It's difficult sometimes. I can't allow personal opinion be a factor in matters of the law. Quite frankly, from a subjective point of view, I didn't think much of you after that unfortunate series of events you were involved in, and I would not have cared if you had gone to prison when you came of age. I was wrong about you. I've been wrong about a lot of things in my life. Some of the things I've been wrong about have proven to be the most valuable lessons I have learned. I honor your perseverance, your dignity, and your intestinal fortitude. Your unwavering work ethic will serve you well." He handed me a business card that had his home phone number written on the back.

While the women were busy cleaning up, the men threw horseshoes and watched the Alabama football game on television. I walked past the group playing cards that included Charlie.

"Roxanne, take a seat. We'll deal you in," Charlie urged.

"Well, maybe just a hand or two," I replied coyly.

I quickly took two pots and then folded a winning hand to give back what I had won and excused myself.

"Better quit before y'all take all this hard earned money of mine," I quipped.

Charlie walked with me a short distance. "Will you see Tom tonight?" He asked.

"Probably. If he's around."

"Do me a favor. Go find Cynthia. She has something I'd like for you to give to him. I think it would mean a lot coming from you."

I found Cynthia inside. We walked out to the car and she opened the trunk. She handed me that old guitar from the barn loft.

"What's this all about Cynthia?" I asked.

"It's between Charlie and Tom Gentry," she replied.

I found Tom and the others charged with the barbecue behind the pole barn. They all stopped and stared when I turned the corner holding that guitar case.

"Tom, Charlie asked that I find you and give you this."

He walked cautiously towards me and took the guitar case. He laid it reverently on the tailgate of his old pickup truck and opened it. He took a handwritten note that was lying on top of the guitar and handed it to Mitchell. Mitchell appeared to read it to Tom before handing it back to him. Tom placed it back in the guitar case. Closing the case, he thanked me.

"Who's that writin'?!" Mitchell sang out loud.

"John the Revelator!" they replied.

The following day, Rory and Collette, along with their parents and Patti, came for lunch before driving Rory to the airport in Birmingham. Rory was leaving for school and was genuinely excited. His parents were extremely proud as was everyone else. I felt as though I was losing a brother, lover, and a friend. As we were all saying our goodbyes Rory made an announcement of sorts.

"Roxanne, I'd like for you to watch out for my Jeep. They will not allow freshmen to have vehicles at school. It's too far to drive anyway."

"I'll take care of the registration and insurance if you take care of the Jeep," his dad laughed and handed me the keys.

"I'll be home for summer. Don't get any bright ideas," Rory joked.

"You've got yourself a deal," I smiled and nodded.

I was busy helping Rory get his things out of the Jeep and moved into his parent's car when he said the strangest thing.

"I believe that in the end there are very few things that will really matter. Knowing you will always matter to me, Roxanne. I know there's a fair chance that we might never see each other again. I will live this summer in my heart from now on. Thank you," Rory said. I could only smile.

Patti and Collette stayed at the Hardwick's with me. They had not planned to make the trip to Birmingham. After drawing straws, I was nominated to drive on the first day of school on. We played Yahtzee and Checkers for a while and then rode into town for a milkshake. Collette and Patti melded into the crowd.

"Did you have fun yesterday?" It was Mitchell.

"I had a blast!"

"I did too," Mitchell said. I sort of lost track of you. I hope you didn't think I was ignoring you. I got sidetracked with that bunch out at the barn."

"I watched and listened. I have never seen or heard anything quite like that," I gushed.

"Not exactly the sort of stuff you hear on the radio I suppose," Mitchell replied. "I'm leaving for Louisiana Saturday. I'll be back in the spring," he said.

I could only nod my head approvingly. It suddenly felt as though everyone except myself was going somewhere. "I hope you'll stop by between now and then," I said, trying not to sound as though I was pleading. "I could use a date for the football game Friday night."

Chapter 6

Education

I found returning to school to be mildly disconcerting. My prolonged absence from the routines of academia magnified my inability to adjust. Working for Charlie at the District Attorney's office was more appealing to me than school. I struggled to remember my class schedule and teacher's names, and routine assignments went uncompleted. As mundane as filing motions and checking court dockets could be, I enjoyed listening to the legalese of the office and followed closely the more interesting cases and the legal precedents used to guide the attorneys and judges at the old courthouse.

As circumstance would have it, there was a long-standing poker game at Judge Thompson's office on Thursdays that I found to be more entertaining and educational than any of my classes. I discovered the game quite by accident when I overheard Charlie talking to Dr. Pettimore one day.

I was quickly sworn to secrecy by Charlie. "It's not a high stakes game. It's just that some members of the voting public might not approve of us playing poker at the courthouse. Matter of fact, it's not much of a card game at all really," Charlie explained.

Given the sheepish look on their faces, it seemed an opportune time to ask for a seat at the table. The regular attendees were Dr. Pettimore, Charlie, Judge Thompson, Headmaster Harley Langston along with Max Halpern, and Bill Danbury. I received a Ph.D. in Humanities and Current Affairs sitting at that table. As stodgy as this group sometimes seemed, they were quite the opposite. Conversations and debates ranged from local gossip to the state of the nation. The war in Southeast Asia was being broadcast on the evening news and its barbarism was transparent to all that chose to indulge their senses. The combined but differing sentiment of protestors and politicians formed a collage that was the mural of the day. Everyone had an opinion. Most common was heartbreak. Détente would provide no absolution. The images would never dissipate. I thought of Travis.

Each had an area of expertise or at least an educated opinion of something that the others found interesting. Charlie and Judge Thompson discussed the law. Dr. Pettimore and Harley Langston discussed education while Max Halpern and Bill Danbury centered on local business and agriculture. I was compelled to listen but not speak. Occasionally the cards would stop being dealt while a discussion on a particular matter was verbalized to its conclusion. Sometimes that conclusion might come from a book in the law library. Others might contribute a more cerebral ingredient. The occasional literary quote from Harley Langston usually silenced everyone at the table. I learned nothing about poker at that table. I wasn't supposed to. I learned something much more invaluable. I learned how and when to interject in the company of men. I discovered that the best way for me to be accepted in a world dominated by men was to allow myself to be independent of them without alienating them. To be accepted meant that I had to leverage my assets in such a way that neither misled nor patronized. I found out that a random act of graciousness in a social environment was more impactful than subservience. I once meticulously cleaned Dr. Pettimore's fedora because I had a sincere sense of admiration for his hats and also because I had lost interest in the game that night. Later that evening Bill Danbury asked me to shine his shoes. I laughed until I caught my breath and then replied, "You must have me confused with someone else, Mr. Danbury."

Once Mitchell left, I became a little more serious about school and adhered to its routine. With the exception of Math, I was generally proficient in my classes and was particularly fond of Mr. Tate's literature class. I joined a creative writing group, and I played intramural co-ed flag football on Saturday mornings. One day between classes, a boy approached me in the hallway. I recognized him as the boy from our shooting blind at Max Halpern's farm. His name was Taylor and he was a freshman at Roebuck Academy. He begged my pardon and proceeded to explain that he knew that I was a senior and he was a freshman, and as he did, he became more and more agitated. He was terrified. I gushed. He was trying to ask me for a date and failing miserably. I stopped him mid-sentence.

"Taylor, do you remember that day in the blind when you asked for my help?" I asked.

"Yes."

"It's just that easy. You just ask. The answer isn't always what we want but until we ask the question we never know."

He gathered himself just long enough to say that he would like to take me to the homecoming dance. Before he could finish saying whatever else was fixing to come out of his mouth I held my finger to my lips and sounded "shhhhhh." At first, I was tempted to tell him that I would give him an answer the next day, but I was afraid he might suffer some sort of unrecoverable breakdown there in the hallowed halls of Roebuck. Knowing that he was too young, I insisted on driving. Collette and Patti accused me of cradle robbing. I thought of it as character building. I was sure to involve Taylor in all of the events leading up to the homecoming dance. The local junkyard had donated an old car for the senior class to smash. They sold tickets for .50¢ to benefit the Booster Club. For each ticket, you got to whack the old car with a sledgehammer. On Thursday, the old car was moved to the junkyard. That same night, there was a big bonfire at Max Halperns' place. The marching band was there, the coaches and student body president made speeches, and the nominees for Homecoming Court were announced. It wasn't something that I would've done on my own but the look on Taylor's face was worth the while.

We had agreed to attend the football game separately since Taylor played in the band. I had told him that I would pick him up at 10:00 pm to go to the dance at the school gym. When I returned to Rory's Jeep after the game, I discovered that it had been rolled and wrapped in toilet paper and white shoe polish was used to paint graffiti all over it. A string of cans had been tied to the rear bumper. I was certain that Collette and Patti were somewhere within eyesight laughing like fools. Not one to dissuade their joy, I drove the Jeep as it was back to the house to dress. Taylor's parents must've made two dozen pictures when I got there. I had purchased a boutonniere for Taylor which I attentively pinned to his jacket. At his mother's behest, he had purchased a wrist-corsage in order to preclude any chance of stabbing me to death with a pin. I was most grateful. With the string of cans in tow, we drove to the gym which had been decorated with school colored streamers and balloons. Taylor was ecstatic. I was envious. All of these people had grown up together. Their parents were all friends. Their relationships with each other were bound by a commonality that was unfamiliar to me. They had all looked forward to this night for a very long time and would remember it always. As difficult as it was not to make it apparent, an unyielding sense of envy hung over me.

"Is it true what they say?" Taylor asked during a break.

"That depends, Taylor. What do they say?"

"They say you're a runner. They say you won't be here long."

"I have to find my place in the world just like everyone else. If that makes me a runner, I guess I'm a runner. What else?"

"I heard some girls call you a whore." I knew the girls he spoke of. They were easy to spot.

"People called my mother a whore. I'm nothing like her. She was mean. She drank a lot. She paid more attention to what man she would bring home next than what her kids were doing. She never did anything to better herself. I guess you have to decide for yourself, Taylor. Thinking for yourself and choosing to believe differently from others isn't always easy but you have to be true to yourself or you're no good to anyone."

The school year was passing quickly. Thanksgiving break was near. Little by little I had been picking out the meat of the pecans I had held back. Tom Gentry had been helping and stored them for me at the feed mill. We would sit and pick nuts and laugh about that day at the wholesaler.

"What you gonna do wit' dem nuts Roxanne?" he asked once they were all picked clean.

"I'm gonna make candy out of them and sell them in town for the holidays," I replied. I explained the recipe of egg whites, sugar, cinnamon and a pinch of salt.

"Gonna take a right big oven to toast all 'dem pecans."

"Yes, sir. I have an idea."

"I bet you do," Tom said, slapping his knee.

Max Halpern's son Matthew ran a small pizzeria in town. My homecoming date worked there on weekends. Matthew had agreed to let me make use of his kitchen on Sunday when the pizzeria was closed. Taylor all but drooled at the idea of helping me in the kitchen. He knew how to operate the oven. That was the main thing. I had purchased several cases of quart-sized Mason jars to put the nuts in when they came out of the oven. I used a large stainless steel bowl and mixed up the egg wash. After the first few batches of nuts, I realized that a) I might not have enough jars and b) This was going to be a long night. By sunrise, we were finished and quite tired. We had put up more than one hundred quarts of the sweet & salty pecans.

"What are you gonna do with these, Roxanne?"

"Well, Taylor, this jar is for you. I'll sell most of them. The rest I'll give away as Christmas gifts." I held his cheeks with my hands and cautiously kissed his cheek and thanked him for his help. We cleaned up the kitchen and shut the oven down. I gave Taylor a ride home.

The holiday season was always difficult for me. Moody and argumentative fell short of describing my discontent. People, it seemed, *tasked* themselves with gift giving and recognition of others in order to fill some void yet ultimately felt deflated rather than satisfied by their efforts.

I had lost touch with most of my friends during the school year. The leisure of summer long since passed, our school activities leaned in opposing directions. I was more likely to show up or participate in a school drama than a sporting event and my work at the courthouse kept me busy as well. Once school closed for the Christmas holidays, we reconvened in the barn loft. Collette and Patti helped me with the ribbons and tags for the nuts I had candied. We made small hand-written labels that said Nuts for Nuts and tied bows around the lids of the Mason Jars. We giggled and drank wine. They teased me about my homecoming date and how dorky I had looked in the recent school play. I teased them about being Ra-Ras. It was a term of endearment for the school spirit crowd. Rory came home for the holidays but we didn't see much of him. He and Patti couldn't keep their hands off of each other long enough to socialize. Mitchell came home as well but it was apparent that our time had come and gone just as the summer nights we shared. I took the candied pecans to the beauty shop, the Circle City Feed and Seed, the courthouse, and anywhere else the townspeople would let me sell them on consignment. After paying Max Halpern for the Mason jars, the endeavor yielded a tidy sum of cash.

I turned eighteen years of age on Christmas Eve. I had agreed to go to candlelight services with Charlie and Cynthia. I loitered outside of the church until I saw Tom Gentry.

"I hope I don't get struck by lightning when I walk in," I joked.

"Stay close by. I ain't got struck yet," He smiled.

Afterward, the Hardwicks had friends over to the house for a gift exchange. I had spent the day with Cynthia making up appetizers and decorating. The men sipped brandy and the women drank egg nog. Collette and I got stoned and giggled as we devoured appetizers. After the gift exchange, Charlie tapped his brandy snifter with a spoon producing a distinctive ring.

"Thank you all for coming tonight. Now there is one more celebration tonight."

Cynthia walked in from the kitchen carrying a cake with eighteen candles blazing on it. Everyone sang Happy Birthday and chanted "Make a Wish!"

I blew out the candles. Dr. Pettimore walked towards me with a small package. "It would be remiss of us all not to acknowledge your birthday," he said.

I stood there holding the package not sure of what to say or do. I was a little overwhelmed.

"Open it up, Miss Roxanne," Tom Gentry insisted.

The package held a leather address book and a journal. Everyone had written their names, addresses, and phone numbers in the book. In the front of the journal, someone had written: "You'll know when you get there." The journal would be the first of many that I would fill and send back to Cynthia Hardwick for safe keeping. They would become the story of my life.

Chapter 7

Gulf Shores

I left Houston Co. Alabama that spring in a 1960 Rambler American I had bought from Granny Gunter for ten dollars. It was as ugly an automobile that anyone could hope for. The paint had become mottled and faded from sitting unprotected, and it looked like a fallen leaf from a tree. The ever-colorful Mrs. Gunter had hated it since the night she caught Mr. Gunter in the spacious back seat dressed in a diaper and being spoon fed breakfast cereal by a Hispanic woman he employed. She had tried to give the car away when the old man died but no one would have it. I insisted on paying for it.

Some say it is a primordial instinct to be drawn to the ocean. I just knew that I wanted to see it. I made the short drive south into Florida until I reached Highway 90 near Chipley before navigating westward. After crossing the Choctawhatchee River, I stopped in Ponce de Leon. I fixed a baloney sandwich from the provisions in the small cooler and ate under a live oak tree at the Ponce de Leon Springs State

Park. A park ranger stopped by. He was polite and we chatted for a bit before he asked if I was going swimming.

"Swimming where?" I asked

"The springs would be the only place close by to swim," he countered.

The blank look on my face must have been a sound indication that I had no idea what he was talking about.

"You've never been to the springs have you?"

The blank expression remained on my face.

"If you like, just follow the signs down at that walkway. There's a bath house down there. Go have a look. You'll like it," he said as he left.

I took a towel from the trunk and walked down to the pathway he had pointed out. The wooden walkway was lined with posts that were joined by a rope that served as a sort of handrail. It also dissuaded curious folks from wandering off into the surrounding wetlands. The canopy muted the bright sunlight. I paused to look and listen. The moss-covered bald cypress trees stood as sentinels over the wetlands. I heard a woodpecker drumming in the distance. A Cooper's hawk dove from the treetops and took a large frog from one of the cypress knees below him. He returned to a nearby tree limb having never touched the ground. I rounded a curve in the walkway and there, where a lone sunbeam had navigated its way through the canopy, and shone on the boardwalk, a cottonmouth lay sunning itself on the warm boards. I passed cautiously as the snake slid off of the walkway on the opposite side. Near the end of the shadowed walkway, the late afternoon sunlight broke over a large opening. On one side, the trees and undergrowth had been cleared by the Corps of Engineers and a narrow man-made beach area lay at the foot of a stone retaining wall. The large pool of water flowed to Sandy Creek which eventually fed into the Choctawhatchee River further downstream. I had never seen anything quite like it. The water was much the color of an aquamarine Crayola Crayon and was clear as glass. The bottom of the pool appeared to be hard packed sand and was void of any vegetation or rocks. I sat quietly on my towel and watched a heron feeding along the narrow channel leading to Sandy Creek. The muffled sound of the water flow made me drowsy. I stretched out on the towel I had brought along and fell asleep in the shade of a tree. I awoke to someone rocking my shoulder back and forth. It was my new found ranger friend.

"There are a couple of yurts not being used in the camping area if you need a place to stay the night. There's no one up there."

"Yurt?" I laughed.

"It's like a tent with a floor only better," he explained.

We walked back to the parking lot together and he pointed towards the camping area. "Thanks for the offer but I'm gonna keep moving," I said.

I traveled south along Hwy 81 more or less following the Choctawhatchee River. Having found the end of Hwy 81, I worked my way west to 79 then south towards the Gulf of Mexico. I had lived within a short distance of the Gulf of Mexico my entire life and thought of what it might be likened to. I quickly realized that my imagination fell well short of reality. I stopped as soon as I found suitable public access. I grabbed a towel and my flip-flops and walked along a boardwalk to the beach. The flip flops quickly proved to be cumbersome in the sand. Their heel would get sucked into the powdery quartz sand, and they quickly came off of my feet. My bare feet squeaked in the bleached white powder. Sea oats danced on the nearby dunes. I watched the shorebirds overhead. Pointed towards the breeze that blew inland, they hung motionless in the opposing wind. I had imagined great waves, but the water was quiet and flat. The water's color was much the same as the springs. The only sound I heard was that of the wind. I waded along the water's edge stopping to pick up the occasional shell or shark's tooth for what must've been a mile before turning back. My lips tasted like potato chips.

I drove west along Hwy 98 to Gulf Shores, Alabama. When I thought of Dr. Richard Pettimore, I smiled. It was getting late in the day when I spotted a food truck near the beach. I had a fried grouper sandwich served on toasted bread with tartar sauce. The girl with the bleached, straw like hair came out to the picnic table where I sat. She appeared to be a few years older than me. Her skin was deeply tanned and leather like. She wore a visor and sunglasses and introduced herself.

"I'm P.D. How's the sandwich?"

I nearly choked when she spoke her name. "Petey?"

"No! P.D. It's short for Priscilla Dianne," she laughed. "Looks like you got a little sun today," she commented. "Be careful not to get over cooked. It can ruin a vacation."

"Thanks. I'll be more careful."

"You'll need sunglasses as well. Your eyes are bloodshot. The reflection off of the sand and water is brutal."

"Are you the Caretaker of the Beach?" I asked.

"No! But I have seen vacationers get overcooked before. It's not a pretty sight. Are you here with your folks?"

"Not hardly. I'm just passing through," I answered.

"I'm fixing to lock this meat wagon up for the night. Want to grab a beer?" she quizzed.

I had no plans and it seemed like an innocent enough offer.

"Sure. Why not?" I answered.

I waited while she locked up.

"I really need a shower. You want to follow me over to my place?"

"Ok."

We drove a short distance to a neighborhood inland. P.D. lived in a garage apartment that was built on stilts.

"Make yourself at home," she said as she opened the locked door.

Furnishings were sparse, but the place was clean and I lounged on a bean bag chair while I flipped through her record collection. I selected Idlewild South.

"Turn it up!" was the shout from the bathroom. I smiled to myself and turned the volume up.

She came out of the bathroom wearing a pair of cutoffs and a halter top as she dried her hair with a towel.

"I love the Brothers," she said with a big grin on her face. "I saw them in Piedmont Park when I was passing through Atlanta on my way down here last year."

"Down here from where? I figured you to be a local."

"Hell no. I'm from Slippery Rock North Carolina," she laughed with a hillbilly accent.

"How did you wind up here?" I asked

"Same as you, only my car is uglier than yours."

We both laughed. I asked if it would be ok if I took a shower.

"Mi Casa, Su Casa," she smiled.

Despite the not so flattering name, The Wreck was actually quite nice. Situated at the end of the jetties that led from the lagoon to the Gulf of Mexico, it offered an amazing view through the expanse of windows. The large saltwater aquariums were intriguing as were the taxidermy mounts of the pelagic species of the area. The Yellowfin Tuna, King

Mackerel, Wahoo, and Mahi may as well have been alien lifeforms. They were all very unfamiliar to me.

"I caught all of those," he laughed.

"Very impressive. I'm going to assume you didn't use red wigglers for bait," I laughed.

"You assume correctly!" He extended his hand and introduced myself. "I'm Griffin. Call me Griff."

"Roxanne," I replied.

We must've looked a little awkward standing flat-footed in the middle of the room talking while everyone else was seated or shooting pool. I had begun to shift from one foot to the other and looking around the room.

"I'm sorry. Would you like to sit?" he asked.

"Actually, I'm looking for my friend that I came with," I replied.

"I'm sorry. I didn't know you were with someone."

Roxanne had started to say something when a voice rang out. It was P.D.

"Griffin Stanley! You keep your distance!"

"Y'all know each other?" he asked, looking at both of us.

"We met today," P.D. replied.

We spent the evening drinking beer and throwing darts and shooting pool. Their fathers were business partners in the Gulf Shores Development Alliance. They were both employed in the family businesses to one degree or another. P.D. preferred the more casual responsibility of the food truck where Griff was charged with various responsibilities at the marina. Together, their parents owned The Wreck and it was there that P.D. held more responsibility than the food truck demanded. As food and beverage manager, it was up to her to assure that both the bar and the restaurant were both well stocked with all that was needed.

"Ladies, it was real but I have got to get some sleep!" Griff announced.

"Griff captains the dolphin cruise at the marina," P.D. snickered.

"Among other things, thank you very much," he replied.

"Can you give Roxanne a ride to my place? I have to close tonight," P.D. asked.

"Uh, yeah. I guess."

We left for the short drive back to P.D.'s apartment.

"What's a dolphin cruise?" I asked.

Griffin laughed. "Well, it's where area guests pay for a seat on a boat and I take them out in the gulf sightseeing. The dolphins know the boat and show up for handouts. In calmer waters we let the guests, a few at a time, get in the water with them. You should come. You can be my guest."

"Seriously?"

"Got something else to do in the morning?"

"Well now that you mention it, no."

"Good. I'll pick you up at 5:30," Griff said.

It was still dark when I heard the knock on the door. Startled, I jumped up and pulled on some clothes to meet Griff at the door. When asked, I told him that I had been up for a while. Having noticed that I was wearing my shirt with the wrong side out, he doubted me. The marina was buzzing with activity when we got there. Shopkeepers were opening their doors. The charter boat captains were loading ice and pumping diesel fuel, and the various information booths and vendors were opening for the tourists that would come seeking adventure. I made my way around the Sea Star while Griff was checking the manifest, loading supplies, and inspecting the engine room. The boat had an enclosed, climate-controlled lower deck with viewing windows all the way around and was complete with a snack bar, restrooms, and an open-air viewing deck on top. In the wheelhouse, I stared at the various required licenses, occupancy certificates, and Coast Guard annual inspection records on the wall. Griffin Stanley's captain's license hung on the wall as well. It had a photo with a seal from the Coast Guard and one from the State of Alabama.

"You want to drive?" was Griff's voice from behind me.

"I don't think that would be a very good idea. Thanks for asking though," I replied.

He had me collect tickets from the passengers and check their names on the manifest as they boarded. I collected the boarding passes and deposited them into the slot of a small metal lock box that was attached to the railing of the boat. Their names checked off the manifest, the (mostly) families with small children boarded and sought out what they thought would be good vantage points for the morning. Once all guests were aboard, Griffin started the big diesel engines that powered the Sea Star and the kids all squealed with delight. The sun had broken the boundary line between the water and the sky, and small points of light danced on the water. I found my way to the upper deck and sat with my legs dangling off of the small observation deck that was outside the wheelhouse. Inaccessible to the passengers, Griff had thrown down a rope ladder I used to clamber up to the small deck. We eased our way out of the marina as Griff navigated the boat through the channel formed by the jetties. By way of the small microphone that was clipped to his shirt, Griffin served as narrator. His voice went out over a series of loudspeakers mounted around the boat. The dolphin cruise, as it turns out, was as much an advertising vehicle as it was a nautical wildlife adventure. Capt. Stanley would notify the passengers of the various points of interest as we passed them and provide a description of their offerings. All of these points of interest were holdings of the Gulf Shores Development Alliance.

Just outside of the channel leading from the marina into the bay, the boat slowed. Griffin's cousin who ran the concessions took over the narration. "Folks, if you'll look around, there is a good chance you'll start to spot some dolphins in this area," she announced.

As if on cue, dolphins started to break the surface not far from the boat. The children squealed with delight and when the narrator announced that there was dolphin *chow* available at the concession stand, mom and dad reached into their pockets and purses. There was a run on the concessions area as they clamored for the opportunity to feed the dolphins and keep them visible as long as possible. Griffin provided an educational narrative for the parents. He spoke of the feeding, breeding, migration, and ecological particulars of the bottlenose dolphins and of their relationship with other oceanic mammals. Feeling validated, mom and dad took pride in their decision to book the cruise. I found the *interactive* experience abhorrable. Griffin throttled up the Sea Star and eased out of the bay and into the Gulf of Mexico. The waters of the bay were relatively shallow and the sandy bottom was covered in various seagrasses making the water appear dark gray, and eventually gave way to the emerald waters of the Gulf once the jetties were behind us. Birds started following the boat. The voice of the girl at the concession stand came back over the speakers.

"Anybody want to feed the birds?'

Another run on the concession stand wiped out the popcorn that the passengers tossed into the air for the birds. The kids who were positioned on the boat in such a way that the popcorn just blew back into their faces cried and those with positions that provided favorable wind direction squealed in delight. When he wasn't laughing hysterically, Griff was on the loudspeaker identifying the different species. He randomly changed directions to afford the opportunity for the crying kids to toss popcorn to the birds. There was a noticeable chop on the water in the gulf. A few of the passengers started hurling their Belgian waffles over the rail. Griff was laughing his ass off as he purposely positioned the boat to maximize the effects of the water rocking the boat. Further offshore, the waters calmed as did the stomachs of the passengers.

Attention turned to the charter boats. We got close enough to see the patrons reeling in fish on the Bertram and Hatteras sport fishing vessels. They held up their catches for the passengers on the Sea Star to see. The masculinity of the men on the dolphin cruise was bruised. This was all by design. In some form or another, all of these vessels were a source of revenue for the members of the development group. The passengers on the dolphin cruise were introduced to sport fishing, timeshare opportunities, local bars, restaurants, and other points of interest by way of narration over a loudspeaker, dolphin chow, and popcorn. I began to laugh.

The coup de grâce came after we returned to the bay and the passengers were afforded the opportunity to enter the water with the dolphins. Wearing life vests, and having been tethered to a 100' length of floating rope, they slipped into the calmer waters of the bay and bobbed in the water while the passengers that remained on board fed the dolphins. Once back on board, those brave souls that had entered the water were held in high regard by the others. How could mom and dad possibly say no when the individualized photos made by the concessions girl were offered for sale once the Sea Star returned to the marina. Once docked, the men headed for the charter boat information booths. The women refereed the kids screaming to buy the rubber dolphin toys and Sea Star t-shirts at the souvenir stand that had been set up. There seemed to be no end to the number of ways money rained down on this place.

Griff came down from the wheelhouse as the passengers were getting off and found me on the lower deck.

"You hungry?" he asked.

"Starving!" I replied.

We drove the short distance to The Wreck and went inside. The cool, dark interior was in stark contrast to being outdoors and was a welcome change. We took a seat and looked over the menu. I ordered the shrimp po'boy and a Coke.

"Half dozen steamed on a house salad?" the waitress asked of Griff.

"Blue cheese dressing and a Coke," he replied.

"What did you think of the dolphin cruise?" Griff asked.

"I found it to be duplicitous and morally reprehensible," I laughed.

"We like to offer our guests a variety of entertainment options and make sure that they know about them," he smiled.

We talked and ate lunch. I told Griffin about my plans. I spoke little of where I came from or how I came to be in Gulf Shores. When asked about family, I spoke only of my grandparents.

"Have you thought about how long you want to hang around here?"

"Not really. Why?"

"Well, we can always use some help here in the summer if you want to work. Of course, if you are the beneficiary of a trust fund and have unlimited resources, you can just hang around for the hell of it," Griffin joked.

"What did you have in mind?"

"Lots to choose from. Waiting tables, timeshare presentations and tours, information booths, souvenir shops. We can always use a good fish cleaner at the fish market. You know, cutting off heads and shoving guts down the chute. All of the charter boat captains are always looking for a master baiter," he laughed.

"Ha-ha. Don't quit your day job Skipper. The kiddies might miss you," I smirked.

"I'll tell you what. Take my car and go do whatever. Meet me back here at 5:00 pm and go out with me on the dinner cruise this evening. I think you'll like it. All adults.

Good money to be made and you're free to do whatever during the day."

"Would I have to sell rubber dolphins and t-shirts?"

"Here. 5 pm," he said and handed me his keys.

The dinner cruise was simply a precursor to a timeshare presentation. Guests were served dinner catered by The Wreck. The assignation of hosts and hostesses to assigned areas assured that the guests had all that they needed. There was no menu, and drinks were limited to beer and wine. The hosts and hostesses were select employees of the Gulf Shores Development Alliance dressed in sequined dresses and tuxedos whose goal was to get a commitment from the attendees to come to a timeshare presentation the next day. The hosts and hostesses were paid a commission for verified commitments to attend but did not participate in the timeshare presentations. The pitch came right after the fireworks display over the bay. Those that committed were given VIP vouchers for the Sea Star's Casino Cruise. Afterward, there was music and dancing as the attendees gradually became inebriated.

We returned to the marina shortly after 9 pm. After the guests staggered off the boat and the cleaning crew came onboard, Griffin and I went to The Wreck. P.D. was working the bar and a hard-hitting band was playing out on the deck stage. I was a little high when P.D. asked me to take some ice to a back room. I made my way down the dimly lit hallway she directed me towards until I reached the large double doors that read Employees Only. There was an attendant there to make sure no one mistook it for a restroom. The room was tastefully decorated; there were no taxidermy mounts or aquariums displayed here. This was a cardroom.

My earliest memories of playing poker were from a very young age. Papa had two regular games he played in. One was at the textile mill, and the other was at the American Legion where Granny played BINGO. He taught me that making money at poker was more than knowing how to win a hand. It was just as much about knowing how and when to lose. The game at the mill was played with co-workers. Some of these co-workers were people he had to report to. He was always careful to lose more hands than he won. The idea, he explained, was to make the hands he won worth just a little more money than the ones he lost. This provided the opportunity to stay in the game for many years, and I was there to watch. On the ride home every week, we would talk about the hands he folded and the hands he won. He taught me to never bet what I don't have. I abandoned that lesson that night in Circle City. I never made that mistake again.

The game back home at the American Legion was entirely different. These players were wild and reckless. Calmer heads like Papa's always prevailed and though the stakes were small, he felt no obligation to appease the other players except when to do so would increase the pot he was about to take down. It was at this game that I learned how to play another person's cards as much as my own. By the time I was sixteen years old, I had won the annual American Legion Poker Tournament sponsored by the Women's Auxiliary twice.

The game at The Wreck was poker at a whole different level and I wanted in the game.

"Screw dolphin cruises," I muttered under my breath.

I took the ice to the bartender. He was a silver-haired Cuban gentleman with a waxed mustache and introduced himself as Elian. When I returned to the bar, Griffin and P.D. appeared to be arguing. Griffin left when he saw me coming.

"What was that all about?" I asked.

"Nothing. Griffin was just being pissy," P.D. replied. "Go have fun. The band is kicking ass, the beer is cold, and if you can't get lucky in here tonight, something is bad wrong with you," she laughed.

Around midnight, P.D. pulled me off the dance floor.

"Time to go," she said, "unless you've got something else in mind."

I could only smile like some slack-jawed fool and followed her out.

I hung out with P.D. at the food truck the next day. She explained that Griffin got worried when I went into the cardroom the night before. "There are people with reputations in that game who prefer not to be identified with illegal gambling," she told me.

"Can you get me in the game?" I asked.

"Hell no! Taking ice to the bar is as close to that game as you will ever get!" she scolded.

"I can handle myself," I countered.

"It's not about whether or not you can play poker, Roxanne. It's much more than that. If you want to play poker you just need to go on the Casino Cruise," P.D. suggested.

On Friday and Saturday nights each week, Capt. Griffin Stanley hosted the weekly Casino Cruise aboard the Sea Star. Some of the well-heeled guests on the Casino Cruise were there because they had been given a *free* voucher from the timeshare presentation they had attended. The others were just thrill seekers. I rarely saw a real card player on the boat and this became my paycheck for the summer. After cruising the bay and nearby shoreline while the guests bought drinks and ate hors-d'oeuvres, Griffin navigated the requisite distance offshore to international waters and BOOM….legal gambling! I mingled among the guests in a cocktail dress I had borrowed from P.D. and watched until I found the right game to join.

One Friday night I had a chance encounter with the bartender from the card room at The Wreck. I had taken a break and was wandering around the upper deck when he saw me.

"If I didn't know better, I'd think you were taking advantage of these good folks." He spoke with a faint yet distinct accent.

"I use what I know to my advantage. If that's what you mean, yes," I replied defensively.

"So I see," he replied.

"Are you here to play?" I quizzed.

"Me? Lord no. I don't play poker. I come out occasionally to make sure everything is on the up and up as they say. I used to play professionally, but the family pays me to keep an eye out for any cheats or hustlers. It's bad for business."

"What about the game at The Wreck?" I asked.

"I'm strictly a bartender there. It's a closed game. They monitor themselves," he replied. "Say, do you have any experience dealing cards?" he asked.

"Just dealing? Not playing? No."

"There's a group of investors from Texas coming into town next week. They are high rollers. It's been suggested to me that I employ a dealer while they are here. I could show you all you need to know if you're interested. They'll be playing with the regulars at The Wreck," he explained.

"I don't know. It sounds kind of boring," I replied.

Elian laughed. "Ma'am, you've never seen cards played like this. It's anything but boring and you might learn something if you pay attention. Besides, it pays well, and I'm sure the tips will be generous. Stop by around lunchtime tomorrow and we'll talk."

I agreed and went up to the wheelhouse to see Griff before returning to the tables.

"Did Elian talk to you about the card game?" he asked.

"He did."

Griffin shook his head and appeared worried.

"Griffin, you don't know me very well. I'm not one to walk into anything I don't think I can walk out of. I've been fooled before, but this doesn't look like anything I can't handle," I said assuredly.

I met with Elian the following day to hear the particulars of the game. He explained who the players were, what their expectations from the dealer might be, and what I might expect. The game would be Friday night following a day of meetings and visits to various properties. Despite the outcome of the meetings, the mood *should* be congenial. The buy-in was five thousand dollars with no limit on betting. Sealed decks of cards were to be used. Breaks were every two hours and a new deck was broken after each break. Alcohol was not to be served at the table but players could bring their drinks to the table after the breaks. I was told to dress conservatively and not to interject unless I was asked to.

"Don't worry. I'll be there all night. You'll be fine," Elian explained.

It never occurred to me that sleeping late and recognizing the time of day only by the setting sun over the Gulf of Mexico might be a suitable lifestyle. I had no illusions that summer would never end or that my wits and charm would afford me an eternal life of leisure, but for now, I was where I was supposed to be. The week leading up to the poker game at The Wreck was no variant. I would occasionally fill in for P.D. at the food truck while she and one of her local boyfriends stole away to her apartment for some privacy; I bummed around the shops at the marina and spent time on the beach. Nearby Fort Pickens was my favorite place to watch sunsets. I had made acquaintance with a National Park Service employee that would let me hang around after the gates closed for the day. We'd gather near the bronze cannons on the top of the fort walls. He was something of an authority on Civil War history and despite my lack of interest in the subject, the tone and meter of his voice was hypnotic as he spoke of the battles fought there and other places in the Deep South. I'd sit mesmerized watching the sunset as the transparent heat waves rose from the cool water as the sun settled at the bottom of the expanse of purple, yellow and orange that was the sky. I felt grounded being away from the rubber dolphins and airbrushed T-shirts.

The night before the poker game, I stopped to watch a fishing charter unload at the marina. The party had just returned from an offshore trip and the hold was laden with Yellowfin Tuna, Mahi and Amberjack .

"Do you like sushi?" was the voice behind me.

"I'm not sure. I've never tried it," I replied. It was all I could muster.

"Don't waste your time," he smiled. "I much prefer a fried grouper sandwich. Know where I can get one?"

"Yeah. The Wreck. Fresh seafood, live music…nice place," I replied

"I know The Wreck. I was there for some meetings yesterday," he said. It was then and there that I realized he was with the investor group from Texas and that I had better put the brakes on.

"Enjoy your stay," I said as I began to walk away.

"Wait. How about dinner?"

"No, thank you. I have some shopping to do. I have an important engagement tomorrow night," I smiled.

I arrived at The Wreck in time for a light meal and to meet briefly with Elian. He told me that the meetings had gone well and that the mood should be light and celebratory tonight. Having finished their meal, the investors and Gulf Shores Development Alliance members filed in and ordered a final drink from Elian before being seated at the poker table. Each player's seat was assigned and marked with a small name placard. I sat patiently looking at the placards and tried to guess which was his. Once they were all seated, I introduced myself.

"Gentlemen, my name is Roxanne Benefield. I'll be your dealer tonight. The game is no limit Hold 'Em. It is my understanding that you all know the game and I can see that you have your chips. I have three sealed decks of cards that we'll use tonight. Breaks are every two hours, and a new deck will be broken after each break. You are welcome to have your drinks at the table but there will be no beverage service during play. Any questions?"

"Is that a new shirt?" he asked. His name was Grady Dalton. "It looks very nice on you."

"Thank you. Good luck gentlemen," I replied, having the only straight face at the table.

Play for the first session was predictably conservative as the players tried to gain some perspective on the tendencies of their opponents. The gentlemen from Texas were fairly familiar with each other's play as were the members of the Gulf Shores Development Alliance. Aside from that, there was a large amount of uncertainty. Toward the end of the first two-hour session, Grady Dalton took down a substantial pot. He had bet conservatively and checked twice to the table before going over the top with a head to head bet against the only other player left in the hand. His opponent folded a flush and he took the pot showing his full house.

"Well done Gentlemen. It's break time. Let's meet back here in 15 minutes." I announced.

I went to the restroom and got a glass of water with crushed ice from Elian and returned to the table. A few of the men had already returned. Some had never left the table. We spoke casually. They asked where I was from and I gave the short version of how I came to be in Gulf Shores. I countered with like questions and posed as generally interested. In fact, I was a little overwrought. I would postulate that these were rich and powerful men. They were educated, and likely influential in circles that extended well beyond small-town politics and social circles. As the night progressed, there was a shift in focus from poker to personal conversation. I was welcomed into the conversations and interjected when I felt it was appropriate to do so. As distracting as it was to me, many topics came up. Some I had a working knowledge and opinion of, others I did not. Despite the huge swings in chip counts, they were able to remain casual and even jovial at times. Three of the players had gone bust and retired to the lounge. I thought of those games at the courthouse in Houston County and the friends I had made there.

The last session of the night was considerably more serious than the others. The remaining three players were studious and methodical. They were anxious for play to end but no one was going to concede. Some of the players that were no longer in the game had returned to the room to see the final play. Grady Dalton finally took the last pot after going all in holding two pairs. When the others folded and showed their cards, the consensus was that he had indeed played well. Either of the two other player's hands would have beaten him. He had not bluffed all night. The men drank and smoked cigars and applauded their week's work and toasted their future successes. Elian came and counted the chips and paid out the cash to the final three contestants.

I went to the bathroom and then headed to the lounge where P.D. and a local guy were slobbering all over each other. Griff and I had a beer and laughed uncontrollably at the two of them staggering around the dance floor. We were interrupted when Elian tapped me on the shoulder and said that the players wanted to see me in the card room. I was handed a cigar and a tumbler of whiskey. Grady Dalton toasted his new associates and then turned toward me.

"Last but not least, I'd like to thank our hostess and dealer. Ma'am, it was indeed a pleasure to have you in our company tonight. I personally wish you all the best and if you ever find your way to Texas, give me a call. I have an eye for talent and there is always room at the table for someone like you in my company." Considerably older than myself, I found him very attractive and somewhat disappointed that his interest in me appeared not to be personal. He handed me an envelope and a business card. The others applauded and responded in kind.

I responded. "Gentleman, I thank you for your generosity and kind words. It has been my pleasure to meet you all and I hope our paths cross again." I spoke briefly to each over the next hour and a half before excusing myself for the night. Lastly, I spoke with Grady. I wanted to gauge his sincerity and to let him know that Texas was indeed part of my travel plan. He insisted that I set aside sufficient time to visit some of his business concerns and consider his offer. I agreed to do so and we shook hands one final time. Elian stopped me on the way out the door and handed me two hundred dollars. "Well done," he smiled

It was quite late and the crowd at the bar had begun to ebb. Griffin was nowhere around and P.D. had made her exit as well. I drove back to the apartment. When I walked in, a pair of boxer shorts hung from a paddle on the ceiling fan. They waved slowly as the fan circled on its spindle. I smiled and fell asleep on the couch. Shortly before sunrise, I heard the toilet flush and a still quite drunken P.D. staggered into the kitchen for a drink of water.

"Do we have company?" I asked

Startled, P.D. said, "Oh hell no! I don't keep 'em overnight."

I laughed and asked about the boxer shorts. "Souvenir?"

"Yeah, I collect 'em," she laughed. P.D. and I became close friends that summer. Much like me, she was vigilant in her efforts to enjoy life to the fullest. One evening she went out to the old fort with me to watch the sunset. Thunderheads loomed in the sky which had taken on an eerie green hue. A waterspout skipped across the bay.

"It's hurricane season. Summer is nearly gone. This is a lonely place when summer is done." P.D. reflected somberly. "The colors aren't the same. It's like the Mahi. In the water, they are a brilliant yellow, blue and green. Once caught, they turn gray and colorless."

I hadn't occurred to me that we would both be leaving soon. She would go back to North Carolina, and I would wind up God knows where. Knowing that it might never happen, I told her I would be back one day and that we'd stay in touch.

"Don't. It wouldn't be the same." She could only smile. I knew she was right.

Labor Day soon passed and the shops and restaurants that existed for summer began closing until the following season. The charter boat captains at the marina pulled up stakes. Some drove overland to Louisiana and Texas to run barges. Others pointed their boats south towards Key West where they would fish the Gulf Stream until the following spring. P.D. and Griffin were busy readying varying interests for their pending closure. There was a private event at The Wreck to mark the end of the season. I attended but felt somewhat out of place. It was great fun and a memorable summer but this was not a place to live. It was a place to visit. I was sitting quietly out on the balcony when Elian approached. He asked what it was that I was thinking about. I told him what Tom Gentry had told me about finding my place in the world.

Chapter 8

Things Aren't Always As They Seem

Harley Langston once told me that the only things Mississippi was good for was Faulkner and separating Alabama from Louisiana. I dallied not in the Magnolia state and soon found myself on the Lake Pontchartrain Causeway. A dense fog shrouded the bridge in the pre-dawn hours and it seemed to take forever to make the twenty-plus mile crossing. I was glad I stopped to use the bathroom and buy gas in Slidell. I had never been in a large city. Once the sun broke and the fog cleared, I realized just *how big* a city New Orleans was.

The Mississippi River drains all or parts of thirty- one states, but it was primarily the sea that deposited the many flavors of humanity into the soup pot known as The Big Easy. The food, architecture, race, beliefs, language, and music overwhelm the senses with their diversity. From the Gulf of Mexico by way of the Caribbean Sea and the Atlantic Ocean in the late 1700s and early 1800s, White Anglos from Europe, Africans, Spaniards, Canadians, Native Americans,

Spaniards, and Haitians consociated to establish what loosely defined Cajun and Creole culture. This was not the South. This was another world. I spent three days just driving around the city. I was charmed by the mansions on St. Charles Avenue as well as the wrought iron balconies of the French Quarter and the shotgun houses of Algiers. Then, there was the food. There was not much that you could dredge up from the Gulf of Mexico or from the swamps and lakes that would not be considered suitable table fare. Whether cooked with fresh seafood or game from low-lying swamps, from savory gumbo and jambalaya to etouffée and pirouges, food was a celebration of life.

There was also a dark side to the city. A history of slavery, organized crime, macabre occult rituals, prostitution, and sneak thievery made up the scar that never healed on the face of New Orleans. Combined with the propensity for flooding and the harsh reality of hurricanes, this was not exactly paradise. I rented a room in a boarding house near the Lafayette Cemetery and worked at a coffee shop in the lobby at the Roosevelt New Orleans. I had never seen anything as visually stunning as the lobby of the Roosevelt. It was hypnotic to sit and watch the coming and going of the well-heeled guests at the Sazerac Bar.

I befriended a bellman that had worked at the hotel since he was sixteen years old. His name was Bertrand Fontenot, but everyone knew him as Shorty. At 6'6" in height, it was only fitting. He reminded me a great deal of Tom Gentry. Now in his seventies, he had seen, among other things, the Jazz Age come and go in New Orleans. I would listen for hours to his stories of the writers and musical artists that he idolized during the 1920s. He spoke also of Prohibition and how it had fostered organized crime in the city of his birth. Modern-day pirates managed to pay off port officials who in turn asked local police to turn a blind eye to their enterprises. He explained how the speakeasies were only occasionally raided in order to feign judicial prudence. During one of our conversations, a young woman close to my age came to join us. Her name was Adele Fontenot. She was Shorty's granddaughter. She had caramel colored skin from Africa, the silky black hair of the American Indian, and the azure eyes of the Acadian. She was the most beautiful woman I had ever met.

"Poppa, are you filling 'dis young lady's head wit' yore sweet talk?" she quizzed.

"Lord, no chile. She's much too clever to be fooled by da likes of me!" he said. "I was just trying to 'splain da difference between Cajuns and Creoles."

Laughing loudly Adele proclaimed, "You mean da difference between a Coon Ass and a Geechie?"

"You know good and well dere ain't no Geechies in Nawlins. Da is all in Charleston," Shorty quipped.

"Whatever you say, Poppa. Unless you plan to study anthropology, don't trouble your head with all of 'dis talk. Cajuns are white and Creoles are black. Cajuns cook with lard and Creoles cook with butter. Dere. Dats all you need to know."

"I'm glad that's all cleared up! My name is Roxanne."

"Adele. Da pleasure is mine."

Adele worked as an escort and freelance model to pay tuition for law school at Tulane. There was no pretense of ambiguity when she told me. I did not ask and she did not share any of the particulars of her work. She suffered no moral quandary due to the nature of her work. The subject never came up again. We lived fairly close to each other and would get together on occasion to visit galleries or to attend lectures but were never particularly close. Between work and school, she had little spare time she would explain. I was a little surprised when she invited me to go with her to Baton Rouge for the LSU vs. Ole Miss game one weekend.

"Bring a nice dress. We'll go out after 'da game," she said. Saturday morning, Adele knocked on my door. "Laissez les bons temps rouler!" she cried out. She was drinking a Mimosa and handed me one. "We're going to go down to da fais do-do and have ourselves some fun!"

Parked at the sidewalk curb was the most hideous car I had ever seen. Far worse than the Rambler, the purple and gold Cadillac was adorned with decals that read Geaux Tigers and was being driven by some poor guy that looked like he'd lost a bet.

"Don't tell me that car is yours, Adele."

"Lawd no child. 'Dat car belongs to my *zanmi*. He's letting us use it for da weekend."

As it would turn out, ours was not the only decadent chariot in this parade. The short drive was rich in flavor when it came to game day travelers. By the time we were halfway to Baton Rouge, I found myself leaning out of the window of the car kissing boys in traffic jams and smoking a cigar as I shouted: "Laissez les bons temps rouler!" or some redneck Alabama derivative thereof. I later begged that the photos be destroyed. Adele howled. Our driver took us straight to a private residence near campus where a large party was being held on the lawn of the property. The bronze plate at the entrance declared the house to be called Nevermore. The house was a Greek Revival mansion with ornate columns. Moss drenched live oaks and magnolia trees lined the driveway. At the end of the drive was a large fountain. A large canvas gazebo was set up with a buffet, live zydeco music, and a number of small bars serving beer, wine, and liquor. The guests appeared to be mostly students and younger alumni. Frat boys, sorority girls, and ordinary students were spilling as much as they drank. The party was hosted by a man by the name of Alonzo Thibodeau. Mr. Tibodeau's family settled in South Louisiana in the early 1800s and made a fortune in a number of endeavors. From cotton to indigo and shrimping, to railroads and trucking, the Thibodeau family held sway in Baton Rouge. Adele and I got separated in the crowd and before long I found myself in need of a restroom. I wandered into the house where I was engaged by Alonzo Thibodeau III. A gangly young man, TIII, as he was known, made up for his awkward appearance with a high dosage of bravado fueled by alcohol.

"Restroom, why yes ma'am. Allow me to show you the way," he proffered.

He led me up a spiral stairway to the second floor then down a seemingly never-ending hallway. "You're Adele's friend. How was the drive up?"

"The drive up was fine. How did you know I was with Adele?"

"She said she was bringing a guest. That God awful automobile you rode up in belongs to my cousin."

The hallway led to the double doors of a bedroom that led to a bathroom that was larger than my apartment.

"Here you are, Madame," he said as he propped himself conspicuously on the marble countertop. "I'll just make sure you have everything you need," he quipped.

Never one to be intimidated, I unzipped my jeans and sat on the commode that was on the other side of a partial wall. When I finished, I pulled the handle and the jet of water that squirted between my legs nearly scared me to death. I jumped up screaming and reaching for my pants. TIII laughed uncontrollably.

"Good Lord woman! Don't you know what a bidet is? Good thing I stuck around or you might've drowned," he said, handing me a towel.

"You're easily entertained, aren't you?" I replied.

"Now, let's not be crass. Aucune blessure madame," he smiled. "Let me show you around and buy you a drink."

We walked back down the stairs and toured the kitchen and dining room. When he opened the door to the library, we both got an eyeful of Adele getting dressed. An older gentleman sat breathless on the leather couch. TIII quickly closed the door before we were seen by either of them.

"How about that drink?" we both laughed.

The crowd in the gazebo had grown rambunctious in the orgy of food, alcohol, and music but quickly dissipated in an organized exit towards the waiting cars for the short ride to the stadium. Adele was nowhere to be seen and I panicked. TIII took me by the arm and led me to a waiting car.

"Don't worry. We'll all meet at the stadium. She'll be there." He assured me.

There was a police escort for the crowd leaving the Thibodeau house that assured the invitees were not detained by something as trivial as traffic, thus missing kickoff. Our car was filled with TIII's friends who were all as queer as he was. The car itself was decaled in purple and orange stripes and was equipped with a horn that sounded like a tiger's roar. The crowd on the sidewalks cheered as our parade passed through the streets tossing out strands of colorful plastic beads and miniature footballs. Once at the stadium, we found our way to the Thibodeau family of VIP suites. I made a comment about seeing the game from the stands and TIII handed me a ticket.

"I'd go too but I have to be here. Adele will be somewhere around this seat. Go have fun," TIII said.

I wandered into the stadium and stopped occasionally to have an usher point me in the correct direction. The fervor through the crowd was contagious. I had never seen a crowd of people in one place that compared. The scene at Tiger Stadium as twilight triggered the stadium lights was epic. My heart raced. I found Adele holding court at the block of seats held by the Thibodeau family. She squealed my name when she saw me. She had reached a state of intoxication that fell somewhere between charming and disorderly. I found an empty seat next to a casually dressed man wearing his hair in a ponytail.

"May I?" I inquired.

"Absolutely," was his reply

His name was Davis. He was a distant cousin of the Thibodeau clan and a student at LSU. When he asked of my affiliation, I explained that I was with Adele.

"Oh, I'm sorry, but I would not be a player in that game," he said.

I took a moment to consider what he'd said and realized that he thought I an escort or *model*.

"No offense," he qualified. "It's just not my thing."

"No offense taken," I replied.

"It's just that...never mind," he said as he stood up. "Please excuse me."

I stood up as well, "Don't go. I'm just here for the game," I noted.

The awkward moment passed and we talked and watched the game. We shared a Jack and Coke pretending that the game had our full attention. There was, however, an increasing physical attraction fueled by the frenzy of the crowd and the whiskey. Halftime came and we walked up to the stadium corridor to use restrooms. When I came out of the restroom, Davis was standing at the top of the steps leading to our seats. He had rolled up the sleeves of his blue-striped oxford shirt to the elbow and was re-tying his ponytail. He reminded me of Rory.

LSU won the game handily and as the crowd began to exit the stadium, I realized Adele was gone and that I had no idea of how to get back to the Thibodeau house. I panicked only slightly but was as soon relieved when Davis asked if I needed a ride.

"Are y'all staying at the Big House?" Davis asked.

"Honestly, I have no idea," I replied only mildly embarrassed.

"I can take you there. It's quite a party. I'll need to shower and change clothes first though."

Just then, a fully intoxicated TIII showed up. "Roxanne, come on. We have a ride to catch. It's party time!"

"How about I meet you there? I'll shower and change as well," I said to Davis.

He stared back looking a little rebuffed. "Sure you will," he said. I put my hand around his neck gently pulling his head slightly to my level and kissed him fully on the mouth.

"Don't dawdle. Get your ass over to the house," I remarked.

When we returned to Nevermore, there was a decidedly different ambiance. The frat boys and sorority girls appeared to have been replaced by a more adult body. The music and lighting were different and I was frightfully underdressed. Adele caught up to me as soon as we returned and handed me my bag, dress, and shoes I had brought up from New Orleans.

"Thank God!" I exclaimed. "I was afraid I might get escorted out of here."

"Don't you worry. Now look, I'll be busy most of the evening so don't panic if I disappear from time to time. You have a good time. You are welcome here and TIII will make sure you don't get into any trouble," she winked.

TIII extended his arm to escort me back into the house. We walked down the long hallway past the library and out of a rear door that led to one of the several small cottages that dotted the property. Warmly lit brass light fixtures welcomed us into the meticulously appointed cottage. TIII led me to a small bedroom and placed my bag on the bed before hanging my dress on the doorknob and setting my shoes on the floor.

"Now come with me," he said.

He opened a door that led into a bathroom lit by scented candles. There was a large garden tub filled with hot water and bubbles.

"Let's get you out of those clothes, Beautiful," TIII said as he reached to unbutton my shirt.

"Wait, TIII. I appreciate the hospitality and you are a gracious host but I sort of have a date meeting me here tonight," I said.

"Well good for you! I hope I get lucky too," he said, smiling mischievously.

He stood silent for a moment and then started laughing the most horrid laugh I had ever heard that ended with him snorting uncontrollably.

"Mon Cheri, you've got me all wrong. I'm as queer as a queer gets. You know 'dat. I'm just here to see that you have all that you require."

TIII helped me undress and led me to the tub. He washed and then rinsed my hair using a garden watering can. He scrubbed my back and my feet. We talked at length as I shaved my legs. That is to say, I talked at length. TIII could pose a question in such a way that the response he solicited flowed as a well-crafted song. By the time the water had grown tepid, I felt like I had met a beautiful lover that I could not have. He wrapped me in a rich terry cloth robe and left me to dress. I felt uniquely beautiful and loved.

Having found my way back to the house, I helped myself to a glass of champagne and sampled the buffet. The plastic cups and paper plates of the pre-game gathering were long gone. The silverware and china along with leaded glass and crystal were quickly and quietly replaced by the wait staff as the guests returned repeatedly for the many offerings. I remembered what Adele had told me about the difference between Cajun and Creole cooking and laughed inside. The beans and rice with sausage from earlier in the day and been replaced by etouffée and shrimp with grits. Papa would've called this: *shittin' in high cotton.* The guests came and went. Some of the attendees, though older and well-dressed, seemed inexplicably nefarious. Small groups of two or three conversed in quiet corners. There were a number of ladies whose role in the gathering was palpable. The queers were blatantly obvious. I felt a little disconcerted even in Davis's company.

Sooner than I could suggest retiring to the cottage, a fracas ensued. I saw Adele at the top of the stairway disheveled and cursing the man TIII and I had seen her with before the game. He followed her down the stairs but kept his distance. Adele stopped to gather herself at the buffet, but when he approached her from behind and tried to take her by the arm, she swung violently and stabbed him in the neck with an oyster fork. TIII came from seemingly nowhere and took Adele into the library, locking the door behind them.

One of the wait staff, a burly black man, took the wounded guest to the nearest bathroom. Minutes later, police and emergency services were outside with lights flashing. By coincidence, a large entourage of the LSU football team showed up at precisely the same time. Swilling champagne and groping women, or anyone they thought to be a woman, they spread like tentacles through the house. One of the players reached up the dress of one of the guests and found things not to be as he had expected. Drunk and disgusted, he slapped the *she-male* to the ground as the guffaw of his friends rose. EMTs attended to the man with the oyster fork in his neck while police interviewed Adele in the library. TIII and a well-dressed woman of a professional persona, who I had not previously seen, sat with her. Two naked men came running through the ballroom laughing hysterically. One wore lipstick and a wig of red nylon hair. When they realized that the police and EMTs were not on the guest list, they quickly ran towards a side door. It didn't take long to realize that once parish police outnumbered the guests and private security that the party was over. Adele's stabbing victim was treated and released. He was advised by police not to press charges as a taxi cab waited outside for him.

Davis and I had stumbled out to the cottage and fell asleep. Shortly before dawn, I woke to a strange sound. I lay on the bed reeking of champagne and cigarette smoke trying to discern what the sound outside might be. As I opened my eyes, I realized that Davis was gone. Near the entrance to Nevermore, lights flashed in the fog that had entombed the moss covered live oaks. I wrapped myself in my robe and stepped outside. Three coyotes were yipping and growling as they tussled with something. I walked towards them shouting and clapping my hands until they ran away. It was a blood-stained dress. I turned toward the flashing lights and walked ever so slowly towards the estate entrance some distance away. I stopped and watched as the fog burned away and was replaced by morning sunlight. As police watched, two EMTs climbed up ladders to remove a body that had been impaled on the spearlike finials of the pickets. When the police saw me watching, two of them began to walk in my direction. Still intoxicated, I panicked and started running towards the cottage. I tripped over a fallen tree limb as they caught up with me.

The parish police led me back to the house and into the library where the others were milling about. The detective in charge explained that there had been a murder and that interviews were being conducted. I recognized the woman that stood by his side as the same that was with Adele the night before after the fork stabbing.

"My name is Virginia Blackstone. I represent the Thibodeau family in various legal matters. You do not have to answer any questions without your own legal counsel nor are you being charged with any crime. I can advise you during the interview if you choose. Do you understand?"

"I do."

The three of us went into a small reading room within the library, and the door was closed shut. The detective spoke after turning on a portable tape recorder.

"Will you please state your name for the record?

"My name is Roxanne Benefield."

"Ms. Benefield, how is it that you came to be at the Nevermore estate this weekend?"

"I was invited by my friend Adele Fontenot to attend the LSU football game as her guest."

The detective made a quick, sharp glance towards Ms. Blackstone.

"Ms. Benefield, are you a prostitute?"

"You do not have to answer that question, Ms. Benefield!" Ms. Blackstone exclaimed.

"It's alright. No sir. I am not a prostitute."

"Ms. Benefield, are you aware of any illegal or immoral activities at the Thibodeau estate last night?"

"Detective, morality is relative only to the beliefs of individuals. Headshrinkers in New Guinea do not think their practices are immoral. As for illegal activities, I was not a victim of or a participant in any such. I cannot speak for the experiences of others."

The detective and Ms. Blackstone looked pensively at each other as the detective removed a photo from a folder he held. It was a picture of Davis.

"Do you know this man?" he asked.

"We met only yesterday and watched the football game together. He was here at the estate afterward."

"Do you know of his whereabouts?"

"I do not. We fell asleep together in the cottage. He was gone when I woke up."

"Ms. Benefield, do you have any plans to leave the State of Louisiana in the foreseeable future? We might have a need to contact you again."

"I have no plans to *stay* in the State of Louisiana but my timeline is indeterminable."

He handed me a business card and asked that I contact the parish office in Baton Rouge should my residency status change. I agreed to do so. I had Ms. Blackstone give me a ride to the bus station and I returned to New Orleans without Adele. I called Charlie Hardwick from a pay phone and explained what had happened in Baton Rouge.

"Yes. Things aren't always as they might seem, are they? New Orleans is a big city with a dark history. Seeing the best in others can cross the line to naivety Roxanne. Therein lays the propensity for trouble," Charlie lectured.

"I was invited to a football game. Why would I have suspected trouble?" I answered.

"Let Judge Thompson and myself make some calls. The answer to your question can most likely be found in the guest list. Call me Tuesday."

"Ok, Charlie, thank you."

I went to work the following day and tended to my business as though nothing had happened. Bertrand was off on Mondays and I was glad. I didn't want to talk about what had happened in Baton Rouge. I neither heard from nor saw Adele and was again comforted. I wanted the whole weekend to just go away. I thought of what Charlie had said about naivety. I worked a mid-day shift on Tuesdays so I was able to call Charlie before I went to work. I forgot that Charlie would most likely be in his office. Instead, I called the house and Cynthia answered the phone. It was obvious from our conversation that Charlie had not spoken of the events of the weekend. I smiled to myself and recalled the premise of attorney-client privilege. Having finished my conversation with Cynthia, I hung up and called Charlie at his office. Charlie explained that he had contacted the District Attorney's offices in both Orleans and East Baton Rouge Parish. Judge Thompson had made some calls as well.

"There was an insinuation that you might be working as a prostitute. When I asked if you were being charged as such, the subject was dropped," Charlie began.

"Charlie Hardwick, you know well and good I'm no prostitute! I am perfectly capable and willing to work. I might sit in on a friendly game of cards from time to time but prostitution, hell no!" I exclaimed.

"I didn't ask or insinuate that you are, Roxanne. I'm just telling you what the conversation was about. Now whether you or anyone else is working as a prostitute is no conundrum to an attorney unless there are charges brought. Since that is not the case, there appears to be no need in discussing it."

"But I don't want you to think," I started.

"Roxanne, I think I know you well enough. Let's just stick to the facts."

"Adele Fontenot is an entirely different subject. Is that correct?" Charlie continued.

I started to explain that which had been told to me when Charlie stopped me.

"Yes, you told me all of that Sunday. The fact is there is no Adele Fontenot listed in the registrar's office at Tulane either as a law student or an undergraduate. She does, however, have an arrest record in both parish District Attorneys' offices for a number of misdemeanor offenses that were reduced or dropped with the aid of a Virginia Blackstone. Ms. Blackstone is a friend and attorney of the Thibodeau family in Baton Rouge. I believe you mentioned meeting her."

"Yes, sir."

"As for the Thibodeau family, theirs is a colorful history going back many, many years. Whereas most of their holdings and business operations *appear* to be of a purely legitimate nature, it has long been suggested that their origins are not of innocent circumstances. From slave trading to rum running to illegal gambling and prostitution, as well as ties to organized crime, the family's past is quite clear and the common consideration of the family is one borne of fear of retribution. Those with close ties to the family that are not blood relatives have been curated through circumstances of quid pro quo. Virginia Blackstone would be one such party."

"Am I in some sort of trouble, Charlie?"

"No. A member of the catering staff was charged with the murder of the young man found impaled on the iron fence near the entrance to the estate. I'd be a fool to speculate on the eventual outcome of the charges. I'm sorry you had to witness all of this," Charlie concluded.

"Thank you, Charlie. I'll call Judge Thompson and thank him as well."

"What will you do now?" Charlie asked.

"I'm not sure. I had planned to stay through Mardi Gras before leaving Louisiana but I'm not so sure now," I replied.

"Well, be careful and stay in touch. Call Tom Gentry at the store sometime, he gets a real kick in the pants hearing your stories. Harley Langston has been teaching him to read," Charlie chuckled. "They use your journal as a textbook."

"Yes sir, I will. I have some more material for the next journal to work on." I smiled with a tear in my eye and hung up the phone. I never knew that Tom could not read.

I did experience the drunken orgy of pagan hysteria known as Mardi Gras some years later but not at this time in my life. I knew there was some religious reference to the celebration but will be damned if I could relate what I saw to anything religious. Many of my plans and their timelines became skewed for different reasons. I drifted through southern Louisiana for some time during a mild winter. The bayous and marshes of the alluvial region were beautiful and wild. The self-sufficient nature of the occupants was characterized by hunting and fishing. Alligator fishing, shrimping, duck hunting, and frog gigging were mainstays of both survival and heritage. Blood feuds between rival family clans were not uncommon, and the order of law was one more of maintaining a level playing field than of enforcement.

I met some locals one afternoon when I stopped for a bite to eat at a small grocery store near Broussard. The Boudreau family ran the grocery store, a fish camp, bait shop, and an abattoir. They bought alligators killed by locals and processed them for meat and sold their hides to leather tanneries. The Sportsman's Paradise nickname for the State of Louisiana was a polite way of saying anything that crawled, swam or flew could be and would be, killed for sport, meat, or trade. Blood was ubiquitous in the sediment of the delta. There was a market for virtually all wildlife byproducts. Feathers, skins, hides, and meat all found their way to the marketplace. It was a visceral lifestyle embraced through heritage. During natural cycles when self-sufficiency was plagued by drought, flood, or disease, the men worked as welders and pipefitters on offshore oil rigs.

There was a screened enclosure with a tin roof that sat on a concrete pad back of the grocery store. There appeared to be some sort of celebration and I was enthusiastically welcomed. I believe they thought I was a distant cousin or something. We ate crawfish and gumbo and passed a jar of pear brandy. I became hilariously drunk in short order and by late afternoon I had fallen asleep in my car. By nightfall, I had sobered up just enough to realize that the invitation to go frog gigging was probably not in my best interest, and I stayed behind.

I was offered a bed for the night in one of the cabins. It was dank and not particularly clean, but there was running water and I had no plans of being there for long. I cleaned up as best I could and brought in a blanket and pillow from my car and fell asleep. During the night, in that state of mind where one is neither asleep nor awake, I heard the door hinge squeak. Instinctively, my eye opened ever so slightly to a slowly widening gap where the yellow glow of a distant light bulb entered. My heart quickened. Suddenly, the door flew completely open and two men rushed in and ran toward the bed.

I rolled off the side of the bed and fell to the floor, but not before grabbing the small .22 caliber pistol that I carried. Quickly on top of me, one tried to hold me down while the other tore at my clothes. I lost my grasp of the pistol in the struggle. One of the men had forced a rag into my mouth so that I could not shout for help while the other pulled awkwardly at my pants. I quieted my mind and closed my eyes as I groped around the floor for the pistol. I pretended to relax and allowed my pants to be pulled off. The two saw this as an act of submission and stood to undress. At that moment, I shot the one closest to me as he was untying his boot, striking him in the butt. The other man howled hysterically as his friend tripped and fell to the floor. I jumped up and pulled the chain that lit the bare lightbulb illuminating the room. The accomplice stood in his drunken, flaccid state and smiled.

"You gonna shoot me too, Red?"

"No, I'm going to have your friend here nail your balls to a tree stump and set it on fire. I'll give you a knife and let you decide what to do with it," I countered.

His flesh wound more painful than mortal, the other man gathered himself enough to get to his feet. "Come on Troy! Let's get the hell outta here before she starts shooting that damn gun again," he said.

Troy took a step towards me and I shot him in the leg. He fell to the floor. Once he stopped thrashing around on the floor, I had his friend tie his feet together using boot laces. Then I had Troy tie the other man's hands behind his back. I pulled up the only wooden chair in the room. I had the guy I had shot in the butt help Troy up from the floor and made him sit on the chair. Then I had him sit on Troy's lap. It looked like a game of Twister.

"Well now, aren't the two of you cute sitting there all shot to hell? Let me tell you sorry inbreeds something. I spent most of my life fighting off drunken sons of bitches like you. You're all alike. You get a little liquor in you and you think that every woman in sight wants you between her legs and that the struggle is just part of the foreplay. I've got news for you. Raping little girls is one thing but you have now officially messed with the wrong person. Here's what we're going to do. You two are going to get your sorry asses into the trunk of my car, and I'm going to drive you to the parish police to confess your sins."

Troy started to contest, shouting vulgarities as the two of them fell to the floor. I was overcome with rage and kicked him in his wounded leg. "Drag your asses to the car!" I ordered.

The two of them made their way out to the Rambler and rolled into the trunk. It was not quite daylight and no one was moving about. The report of the little .22 short was not much more than a pop and the cabin was some distance from the grocery store. No one was the wiser for what had happened. Once I began to drive, I became scared and uncertain of what to do. My greatest concern was showing up at a local law enforcement location only to find it run by the cousins and uncles of the two would be rapists in the trunk of the Rambler. There could be no happy ending to that story. Instead, I started driving toward Alexandria. By the time I got there, the welts and bruises on my upper arms and legs were quite apparent. My lip was cut and I was only half dressed. I followed the hospital signs to the first medical facility I could find and ran into the emergency room. It was fortuitous that a police officer was there. I ran pleading with him and explained that two men had tried to rape me. He had a nurse take me back and clean me up. The doctor came in and examined me. Aside from the bruising and cut lip, I was fine. I just wanted the police and medical personnel to see my condition. I had a contusion on my leg that was shaped like a hand. I wanted no denying my accounting of what had happened and needed validation. After their examination, the police officer came into the examination room and began to make some notes as he interviewed me. When he asked if I might be able to locate and identify the men I nearly fell apart. It was all I could do not to laugh.

"Yes, sir. They are outside in my car."

"In your car? What the hell?"

"I apologize officer. I was hurt and scared. I didn't know what to do. I didn't want them to chase me down and I didn't want to go to the local authorities for fear that there might be some bias there. Besides, they need medical attention as well. I shot both of them."

By this point, the young police officer's disposition was obviously one of confused anxiety. He radioed his dispatcher and within a few minutes, myself, three police officers, and an EMT were all poised at the rear of my car listening to the two men thrashing around inside. I opened the trunk and they squinted at the sunlight until their eyes adjusted and the policemen pulled them out. The EMT helped untie them but not before they were handcuffed and escorted to the ER. As a precaution, I was placed in the back seat of one of the police cruisers and given a blanket. They returned about an hour later.

"Well, the good news is that neither of them is hurt very badly. Those little .22 shorts lodged in the muscle tissue and were easy enough to dig out. Blood loss was minimal. They'll have a pretty good bruise and some scarring but that's about all," the senior officer began.

"Begging your pardon, the welfare of those two heathens is of little concern to me. They tried to rape me. Remember?" I fussed.

"Well, maybe you should be worried, ma'am. Shooting someone is pretty serious even if it's in self-defense. Trust me when I say you don't want to know what it's like to kill a man."

"I feel the same way about rape. Now can I go?" I asked.

"Do you not want to press charges?"

"No, sir. I just want to leave Louisiana. That is, of course, unless those two are planning on pressing charges."

"No, ma'am. They haven't mentioned pressing any charges. I think they've had enough of you for one lifetime," the officer chided.

"Well, sir. I appreciate your help and bid you farewell if we have no further business."

Chapter 9

Austin

I left Alexandria and drove to New Orleans to settle my affairs. I went to the coffee shop at the Roosevelt New Orleans Hotel and picked up a paycheck. I was more than glad to forfeit any further wages I was owed. The following morning, I gathered my clothes and personal items and agreed to a pro-rated amount due for rent. I contacted the District Attorney's office in Baton Rouge and notified them that my residency was changing and if they needed to contact me regarding the events at the Thibodeau estate they could contact Charlie Hardwick who would serve as my attorney.

I felt mildly relieved when I saw the road sign for Beaumont, TX. I stopped at the Texas State Line Welcome Center and took a short nap. Once awake, I showered and changed clothes. I walked into the main lobby of the facility to get a roadmap. Inside, there were travelers getting souvenirs and snacks. I wondered where they were from and where they were going. I went in and took a look at the taxidermy exhibits on display. The roadrunner, armadillo and pronghorn displays reminded me of The Wreck and the fish mounts I saw there. I was looking at a large wall map that noted the various geographic regions of Texas when a couple near my age approached. He had longish hair and wore a floppy leather hat. She was very plain but naturally attractive with long straight hair. She wore a halter top and cutoffs. Both of them wore leather sandals.

"Where you headed?" she asked

"I'm not sure," I replied. It was only then that I realized I truly had no idea.

"Far out," she said. "We're drifting too. We're going to Brownsville then down to Monterey.

I nodded dispassionately. "I think I'll stay on *this* side of the river," I noted.

"I hear Austin is a blast," he pointed out.

"Yeah?" I quizzed

"It's a hip college town with a big music scene," he said. "Be cool little sister."

"Austin it is," I whispered under my breath.

I answered a local advertisement when I first arrived in Austin and rented the little carriage house behind a large home just off campus. The house belonged to a scholarly gentleman I would know as Professor Tidwell. Employed by the university, he served as Head of Integrative Biology at the College of Natural Sciences. We would sit and talk about his now grown children, music, books, and dreams realized or not. He had an 8mm projector and would show me films he'd made over the years. His favorites were from a trip he had made to witness the great migration on the Serengeti Plains of Africa. After Longhorn home games on Saturdays, Professor Tidwell hosted friends, family, and alumni at his home. There was a card game, and with some coaching, he became a pretty good player. It was during one of these games that one of the other teachers asked if I had considered taking some classes.

"No. The thought of sitting in a classroom makes me break out," I laughed. "I was never comfortable in a classroom setting. I can't explain why,"

"College is much different. I think you might be surprised. Perhaps you could audit some classes to get a feel for it," he suggested.

"I'm not sure what you mean," I replied naively.

"To audit a class you need only be registered as a student. First, you must get permission from the professor of the class you are interested in. Once you clear that hurdle you attend the class like anyone else. You don't pay for the class and you do not get credit for having taken the class. There are no assignments to complete and you're not tested on any of the material," he explained.

"I'll certainly give it some consideration. That is indeed *different*," I said.

I called Dr. Pettimore and asked him about auditing classes. He was ecstatic. He said that he would contact the Registrar's Office on my behalf and streamline the registration process for me. He agreed that it was an excellent introduction to what secondary education had to offer. Over the course of time, I would go on to take a number of classes at the University of Texas. I even took Wildlife Biology from Professor Tidwell. I took Literature and Composition, Drama, Business, and Marketing. At Charlie's behest, I even attended some classes at the Law School. I tried not to be disruptive in class but admit that on more than one occasion, my natural lack of ability to restrain myself from voicing an opinion or observation got the best of me. I was known to challenge faculty in what I viewed as a constructive manner. I found out years later that Dr. Pettimore and Headmaster Harley Langston, having been tasked by Charlie, had made it possible for me to pursue my interests in the manner that I chose and had, on more than one occasion, ran interference between myself and the faculty when my *constructive* arguments leaned more towards *obnoxious behavior.*

Austin was a mishmash of seemingly conflicting cultures that had managed to find a way to co-exist. I found this to be the case for much of the Texas that would become my home. Despite its size, Austin maintained the feel of a small town in a progressive and modern culture through diversity. As the state capital, influential politicians and businessmen were plentiful. Home to the University of Texas, Austin was also a college town. Most notable was the epoch taking place in the city's cultural district just across the Colorado River from downtown Austin. Throughout Austin and much of Texas, the hippy and the redneck, the politician and the student, the businessman and the drop out all found a way to co-exist. Austin might not have had a monopoly on this renaissance, but the city was certainly ahead of the curve. At its core, music was the great equalizer. Bars, music venues, galleries and coffee shops morphed out of everything from old National Guard Armory buildings to defunct skating rinks and abandoned brick warehouses.

Well-known artists were known to perform impromptu on a regular basis, fanning the flame of popularity held by the area. I was drawn to this. I became friends with a number of artists in Austin. Most were broken drifters that just wanted to be heard. They would play for meals and drinks anywhere. Some gained a great deal of notoriety among business owners, promoters, and law enforcement. Some honed their craft well and were rewarded with publishing contracts while others became performers and studio musicians. Some would spend time on my couch. Occasionally, one would share my bed. The man or woman that could string together a handful of words that told a life's story was very nearly hypnotic to me. I'll always remember the night that I heard one such person sing Your Cheating Heart. I had heard the up-tempo production of Hank Williams' song many times on Papa's transistor radio but this was different. In the low light of a cocktail lounge tucked away in the corner of a bowling alley, I heard the sound of despair.

I worked afternoons and early evenings for tips at The Hill Country Cattleman's Club. It suited me well. The hours were flexible and my clientele generous. There was an antique barbers' chair of mahogany and red leather accented with brass hardware tucked discretely behind a maroon velvet drape. My clients would sit quietly while the hot towel softened their skin as I sharpened my razor on the cordovan strop that hung from the arm of the chair. I would meticulously apply the hot lather and shave their face and neck to a crisp, clean finish. Conversations were often intimate but never provocative and sometimes included topics related to business or politics. I spoke in a soft voice and worked in close proximity. A nuanced gentleman once told me that he came to see me because the experience was more liberating than a Catholic confessional and sexier than a New Orleans whore house. It was meant as a compliment of sincerity and I took it as such.

One night as I was leaving, a familiar face walked into the club. It was Grady Dalton. We had met in Gulf

Shores at the card game held at The Wreck. "You were supposed to call me," he opened.

"I have it on my to-do list," I laughed.

"Meet me at the Driskill Hotel at noon tomorrow. I have a short trip to make to Marble Falls. We can have lunch and ride out there together," he insisted. I agreed.

Having gotten a little lost, I arrived later than I had planned. Grady had ordered an appetizer and stood when I approached. As the gentleman I remembered, he pulled my chair out for me to be seated.

"Well, Ms. Benefield. How the hell are you?" he laughed. "I apologize for not taking the time to talk last night," he began. "I'm only in town for a couple of days and had to catch up with some folks. I hope you understand."

"It's quite alright. We'll start over," I laughed. "So what's in Marble Falls, Mr. Dalton?" I asked.

"The Los Brazos Hat Company," he replied sheepishly.

"Ah. Shopping for a new hat?"

"Not hardly. They never seem to look right on my head. Actually, I own the company. It's been in the family for a number of years," he responded.

"Now who's embarrassed?" I thought to myself. "I've always thought a fine hat to be the perfect finishing touch," I said.

"Unfortunately the right hat doesn't seem to exist for me. We manufacture raw blanks for private labels. We also distribute finished hats wholesale to retailers under the Los Brazos brand name."

It occurred to me that I had no idea what he was talking about. I never considered how a hat was made. I could not form a mental image of what the process must look like. I didn't know what a blank was and the term private label meant nothing to me. We spoke briefly about his other business interests. He always turned the conversation back towards me. He was never disingenuous. I spoke of the classes I had taken and of the people I had encountered since we first met in Gulf Shores. The drive was short and we soon arrived at the Los Brazos Hat Company outside of Marble Falls.

"I'm meeting with the plant manager and some buyers. If you're interested, you're welcome to join us," he said.

"I'd rather see how hats are made. Can you have someone show me around?" I replied.

"Absolutely! I have to warn you though. It's hot, dirty, and not very glamorous."

"I'll manage as best I can," I laughed.

The felting process was done in a building separate from the rest of the facility for a good reason. The raw material for felt is animal fur. Sheep's wool, beaver fur, rabbit fur, and even buffalo and camel hair could be processed into felt. It was an ancient process. It was a hot, smelly process of heat, moisture from steam and chemicals, and pressure that produced the layers of felt that were folded, pressed and steamed into triangularly shaped cones. The soon to be hats then went to the main production area. The cones were subjected to more heat and steam and fitted over ancient wooden blocks until they began to look like hats. They were then dyed, waterproofed, lined and trimmed in the finishing area. Hatters steamed, shaped and groomed the hats prior to final shaping, cutting, creasing and curling. The hats were sprayed with shellac to stiffen their shape before being boxed and shipped.

I met Grady in the showroom where he was showing some new products to buyers. I walked around casually reading the informational documents on the various hats. Materials disclosure, size availability, colors, and specifics such as brim width and crown height made up the information included in the documents. An accompanying pamphlet outlined wholesale pricing. I took a sand-colored fedora from its stand and tried it on. It was a beaver felt hat with a pinch front and teardrop shaped crown. I was looking at myself in the mirror when I realized the hum of background conversation in the room had stopped. Everyone in the showroom was staring at me.

Startled, I said, "I'm sorry, I didn't mean to interrupt." Grady looked at me standing there wearing that man's hat as though he finally recognized me as a woman.

"No apology needed. Folks, I'd like for you to meet Roxanne Benefield," Grady stated. "Ms. Benefield and I met when I was in Gulf Shores on business sometime back. I hope to find a suitable spot in my business for her at some point. What did you think of the hat making process, Roxanne?"

"I was thinking," I began. "What size hat do you wear Grady?"

"Well, I measure a 7 $3/8$, but hats don't look right on me. I think I mentioned that on the drive over," he said. He seemed a little abashed.

"I can certainly relate to that," one of the buyers chimed in.

"I'll be right back. Please excuse me," I said.

I went with a member of the office staff to get two 7 $3/8$ hats from the shipping area. One was a fedora and the other was a western style hat. I had Grady sit and I carefully placed the fedora on his head before standing back and taking stock of its appearance. Grady's head was true to the size he stated and went on easily but did look awkward.

"I think a man's hat should fit low on the forehead and just above the brow of the eyes and the top of the ears.

Grady, your hat looks as though it's too small but it is the proper size. The problem lies with the height of the crown. I was noticing that the crown height in most of the fedoras varies very little. Head shapes, however, do vary. Let me show you."

I had him remove the hat. I placed a book level on the top of his head and using a ruler, measured the distance from the book to a point just above the brow to indicate the height of the crown of his head. "This hat has a low profile 4" crown and once it's shaped and creased you lose part of that. So the hat looks as though it's sitting on top of your head rather than fitting *over* your head. You have a high crown," I commented.

The other hat was an open crown western hat. The 6" crown and the 5" brim made him look like an old west hangman or undertaker.

"I'm sorry but this is just awful," he squawked.

"It's fine. I'll be back. You get back to your guests."

I took the hat to the finishing area and asked one of the hatters to help me. He was an older Hispanic gentleman that I had met earlier. I had him remove the Concho hat band and rooster feather. We steamed the hat and trimmed the brim and shaped the crown to a shallow center crease with side divots and put on a tasteful wide ribbon band with a less ostentatious feather embellishment. The front of the brim was sloped gently downward and the back slightly upward. I returned to the showroom a couple of hours later as drinks and hors-d'oeuvres were being served.

"Your new hat is ready sir," I announced.

Grady placed the hat on his head and walked over to the full-length mirror that hung on a wall in the showroom. He looked from side to side in the mirror as the others watched.

"I'm never taking this hat off!" he exclaimed. The others applauded.

"How in the world did you make a new hat? Where did this come from? This isn't in our line!"

"It's the same hat you tried on earlier. I just modified it a little," I replied.

"Well, I'll just be damned, Grady! I believe you have found yourself a new hatter!" one of the buyers exclaimed.

Grady, who was normally somewhat reserved, could not stop talking on the ride back to Austin. He was going on and on about his various business interests when I interrupted him.

"What are your plans for tonight? I'd like to take you out."

"No plans. I'll go back to San Antonio tomorrow," he replied.

"There's one condition. No talk of business, and keep an open mind," I demanded.

"That's two conditions," he said.

"Dress down and wear the hat," I said. "Now, there are three."

Friday nights in Austin were exciting. I had been in town for quite some time and discovered that one never knew who might turn up in the clubs. Having a reputation as something of a muse, I had gained privileged access to clubs and artists. I called a couple of people and arranged to get us in at The Armadillo World Headquarters. Jerry Jeff Walker was playing as was Guy Clark. I made my way around the usually off-limits sections of the old National Guard armory building with Grady in tow. Eddie Wilson had provided all-access badges for us. Regardless of how casual the setting might be, I was always careful not to impose on artists. I was content to watch and listen to the language of the craft. It all seemed a little foreign to Grady, but after a few tequila shots, he found his own groove. We got separated briefly and when I caught up with him, he was sitting offstage staring intently as Townes Van Zandt sang If I Needed You. He had agreed to fill in because JJ was predictably late. Before the night was over, a number of other artists had shown up. Various combinations of artists took the stage while others entertained themselves and each other off stage. Grady stayed close to Townes all night. Townes had a way of drawing strangers in. There were many of us that thought we knew him, but no one ever seemed to be able to draw him out of his dark side.

As dawn neared, Grady and I left the club. Our ears were ringing and we were both hungry. I drove Grady's car to a diner outside of town where we had breakfast. After breakfast, we drove out to Dripping Springs. Before Willie Nelson held one of his annual Fourth Of July Picnics there, Dripping Springs was just another small town outside of Austin. The Chamber of Commerce called it The Gateway to the Hill Country. Those of us that walked on the other side of the street called it heaven. Hamilton Pool was home to a grotto formed when the dome of an underground river collapsed exposing the limestone bedrock below the chaparral. The fifty-foot high waterfall on Hamilton Creek fell to a pool of jade green water that even during the hottest days of summer was frigid. Large groups of young people gathered there on weekends. Clothing was optional for those that braved the cold, clear water for swimming. Cannabis was common. This particular summer, there was an encampment of button heads outside of town. They called themselves The Rainbow Coalition. There was little talent in their lot but they viewed themselves as artists. They would tie-dye t-shirts, weave macramé plant holders, string wooden beads on strips of leather, and bake *special* brownies. They would set up makeshift kiosks to peddle their wares.

Grady and I got separated for a bit when I went to find a private spot to pee. On my way out of the brambles, I ran into some friends and stopped to visit for a minute. I roamed around until I found Grady in a drum circle with a djembe. It was hilarious. It was not a Grady Dalton with whom I was familiar. It all made sense when he offered me a brownie.

"These are sooo good," he said. "Kind of expensive though."

"Let's save these for later, ok?" I implored. "Too much of a good thing is *not* a good thing Granny always said."

"Let's go swimming," he said.

He gave the djembe back to his new friend and walked towards the water's edge. Soon, naked as a newborn, Grady leaped from the escarpment into the pool below. I was carried back to the Party at the Pond in Circle City and stripped down to my bra and panties to follow suit. After a few minutes, we climbed out onto the warm rocks to air dry.

"Close your eyes and count how many different sounds you hear," I challenged.

We sat silently for a few minutes. As if on cue, we both raised our heads up and opened our eyes at the same time.

"I heard a dog barking," Grady started.

"I heard two different dogs. One was over this way and one over there," I replied.

"I heard people talking and laughing."

"Were they men or women?" I asked.

"Some of each I think. Did you hear any birds?" He asked. "I did."

"I heard a hawk screech way up high." I looked up into a blue sky, "There. I can barely make him out. He's riding the updrafts. Circling. See him?"

"I gave my hat to that guy last night," Grady said.

"Townes? I thought that hat looked familiar," I laughed. "We'll just have to get you another one."

We pitched horseshoes and threw Frisbees all afternoon. A group of students brought a badminton set and we joined in their games. Grady spotted a young girl struggling to fly a homemade kite and went over to help her. I watched from the shade of a cottonwood tree as they coaxed the kite to take flight. Slowly, but surely, they got the kite pointed in the right direction and it quickly rose in the late afternoon currents of air until it reached the end of the ball of string it was attached to. I walked over to where they sat watching the kite. The girl's mother had joined them.

"It's getting late, Katie. We need to be going," she said.

"Ok mom," the young girl replied.

"I'll wind the kite in for you," Grady started.

"I always set them free. That way somebody else can play with it one day," Katie said. "Just let it go."

Grady looked at me and I nodded. He let go of the string and we all stood and watched until the little kite was completely out of sight. The little girl clapped her hands and squealed with delight. I made a note to the hour of the day and explained that I needed to get back to work. "I wouldn't worry about that," Grady said. "I know the owner."

"That might be, but my creditors might take exception," I laughed.

"It's not the end of the world if I'm not back in San Antonio tonight," Grady explained. "I heard there is a star shower tonight. Let's go back to Austin and have dinner. We can change clothes and come back here later."

As I had thought Grady had no personal interest in me when we first met in Gulf Shores, I was now worried that he did. This would be no quickly passing romance. He looked at me in an entirely different way. I was afraid of commitment. Dr. Pettimore once said so and I scoffed at the suggestion. He was right. It was the reason that I ran. It was also the source of my fierce independence. I had always been afraid that if I committed myself to someone, I might be disappointed or betrayed. I feared also the possibility that I might lose my individual identity.

"Let's just have dinner. I have classes tomorrow and I have to catch up on some reading," I suggested.

I was determinedly enthusiastic when engaging in dinner conversation lest Grady would feel that I had brushed him off earlier. I sat close to him in a booth at a little Tex-Mex restaurant that I favored. We drank draft beer and ate tacos. Every time Grady tried to talk business, I'd talk about some book I had read. When I talked about traveling, he'd ask about family. It was a real standoff. I finally let down my guard and spoke to the life that I usually kept surreptitious for fear of what others might think of me. I told him everything.

"It was suggested that my grandparents were poor. I didn't get it. Still, I don't." I began.

They lived in a small frame house on what I believed to be the most abundant, fertile, and beautiful seven acres of land on the planet. During the summer and over the Christmas break, a parade of overnight stays by me and my numerous cousins was common. There were indoor games, outdoor games, snipe hunting, gardening to be done, and the occasional ass whooping facilitated by a switch off of that damn willow tree out by the road. There wasn't much grass in the yard and Granny could sometimes be seen broom sweeping the hard sandy space in front of the porch where we scratched out hopscotch boards. Markers were bottle caps, stones, marbles, and broken pieces of glass. There was a barn with a hayloft that was overrun with cats, and there was always a new litter of kittens. There was a garage and a workshop outside and a quilt closet inside the house. In the evening, the focal point on cold winter evenings was the fireplace. We burned coal in that little fireplace. The coal was dumped off of rail cars in town. We'd load the coal in the old Dodge pickup truck. Papa would let me stand in front of that fireplace warming my backside for just the right amount of time before gently tugging the front of my jeans at the knee. This pulled the back of my now toasty jeans against the back of my legs. He thought that was the funniest damn thing in the world. Granny dipped Bruton and Dental Sweet snuff and would occasionally lean forward in her rocker, creating a Y shape with her index and middle finger used to part the corners of her mouth to better expectorate a brown stream into the fire.

Summer's canvas was painted differently to suit the season. My grandmother loved to fish. She would fish in a ditch on the side of the road after a hard rain. Her species of choice was catfish and the preferred bait was dough balls. My grandmother would sit for hours watching the numerous lines she had set out in hope of catching something for the frying pan. Sometimes we did. Sometimes we didn't, but it didn't matter. Sometimes, after fishing, she would take me to the American Legion for BINGO. Granny was more excitable than Moses with the tablets of stone marking those BINGO cards.

There was always food. On the stove top in the kitchen, there was a quart-sized aluminum tin with a wire strainer that held bacon grease until it was needed. Biscuits were rolled out from a big wooden bowl that, to my knowledge, was never washed, and was always covered with a dusting of flour. I recall dressing in overalls and long-sleeved shirts and held bacon grease shooed into the blackberry bushes to gather fruit for pies, jams, jellies, and preserves. The clothes were supposed to help keep away the chiggers but rarely worked. We would also gather huckleberries. Huckleberries are a wild strain of blueberries. I haven't seen any in a number of years. My favorite wild fruit was green plums. There was a plum bush that would bear so much fruit that the branches would often split from the trunk. It was always a race between me and my cousins to see who could first gorge themselves on the yet ripened fruit. Armed with a shaker of salt, we would savor for hours on end the tart, sugar-laden fruit until our tongues were raw.

Then there was the garden. It took my grandparents, all of my aunts, uncles, and cousins to keep that garden picked during the summer. There were tomatoes, corn, okra, cantaloupes, beans, potatoes, peppers, cucumbers, and squash. It took another army to can and preserve the bounty. The sandy loam soil had a high saline content that was perfect for the Big Boy and Beefmaster tomatoes. My favorite was digging potatoes with the hand cultivator. It was a lot like hunting Easter eggs. We would eat corn raw off the cob and dinner was often a tomato sandwich. Thinly sliced tomato on white bread with mayo and ground pepper. Supper was a mixed bag of all things grown in the garden and breakfast consisted of fresh eggs and biscuits with syrup.

It was late and the restaurant was closing. "Take a look at your schedule and see when you can spare a few days," Grady suggested. "I'll show you the Texas I know. I wouldn't want you to strike out for parts unknown having seen only Austin and the Hill Country.

Chapter 10

An Idea

Grady:

I knew that I was walking down a slippery slope with Roxanne. We were very different. Nonetheless, I was in love. I loved her not for what I thought she might become but for what she was. I had never met anyone so fearless. My life had been privileged and sheltered. I had never known neglect or misfortune. Likewise, I had never had to rely on my wits to survive nor had I experienced the satisfaction of having done so.

I made the short drive to San Antonio for what was supposed to be a three day weekend with Grady. His home was in the Alamo Heights neighborhood of San Antonio. The house had a slate tile roof and a stone veneer exterior. A large hand-hewn door beneath the copper clad portico led to the open space inside. It was a timber-framed structure with heart-of-pine flooring. Western-themed oil paintings, framed rodeo posters, and Remington statuary accented the great room.

"Have you ever considered painting that car?" Grady asked.

I laughed out loud. "What? Diminish that fine patina? I'd rather color my hair!"

There would be no more Mexican standoffs. Grady showed me to my room and I returned to the kitchen. He was out on the patio grilling steaks and steaming fresh asparagus and corn on the cob.

"I'm glad you came," he started. "We've got a lot to do and see this weekend."

"Business or pleasure?" I asked.

"Travel and sightseeing will be our itinerary. I remember that you wanted to see Texas from "*Houston to El Paso*", so I thought I'd help you with part of that. You can cover more area in a plane than a Rambler," he laughed.

The following morning, we loaded our things into his truck and drove out to Stinson Municipal Airport. I was sweating profusely and my heart was racing. I was nervous *and* excited. "I've never been on a plane," I confessed.

"You'll be fine," he assured. "I've been flying for quite some time. My dad flew and insisted that my brother and I learn as well. It's fun. You'll like it."

"You mean YOU are flying the plane?" I asked with my mouth gaped.

"Would you rather fly with a total stranger?" he laughed.

"I guess not. It's just a little unexpected I suppose."

"We can make a few passes close by to get you used to it. If you feel uncomfortable, we can always drive," he assured me.

We parked near the hangar and unloaded our bags. The attendant at the hangar had fueled the plane and handed the log book to Grady. He looked over the documentation to make sure that everything was current on the plane and did a pre-flight walk around. I thought about Rory.

"I'll be right back. I have to file this flight plan with the tower and we'll get started."

Grady got me seated and strapped into the twin prop Cessna before boarding himself. Once in the cabin, he fitted us with headsets that reduced noise and allowed us to talk to each other. "It can get a little noisy," he had pointed out. He gave me the cursory overview of the instrument panel once he powered up the electrical system. He pointed to the gauges that indicated the critical functions and noted that their readings were what they should be. I exhaled deeply and he started the engine. We taxied the short distance to the runway while Grady communicated with the tower over the radio. Once cleared for takeoff, Grady throttled up the engines and we rapidly gained speed down the runway. The plane lifted gently off the ground and rose slowly. "Look over to your right," Grady said. That's Austin."

"But we just got off the ground!" I exclaimed

"Like I said, you can cover more ground with a plane," he laughed.

Grady pointed the plane west and we flew a short distance above the Colorado River towards Marble Falls and Lake Lyndon B. Johnson. Having turned back to the southeast, Grady pointed out Dripping Springs. "Are you ok or should we land?" he asked.

"I'm with you," I smiled. With the increased speed and altitude, the flight to Alpine – Casparis Municipal Airport took little more than 2 hours to complete. Along the way, Grady insisted that I try my hand at the controls. I politely declined. He kept an old jeep at the Alpine airfield that I loaded our things into while he checked in and gave instructions to the hangar attendant. "Have you ever been river rafting?" Grady asked.

"I can't say that I have," I replied.

"You'll love this," Grady said.

We drove south from Alpine into the Chihuahuan Desert. Occasionally, Grady would take the jeep off road for a more intimate view. I had always imagined a desert to be a stark, lifeless landscape. As with many other things, I was wrong in my thinking. The blue sky was likely to be interrupted by a butte painted in hues of umber and sienna before giving way to a grey and green floor of lichens and cacti and finally a meadow of wildflowers. Dense areas of buffalo grass were dotted with mesquite and barrel cactus. With its bulbous eyes protruding from the side of its head, the pronghorn was unearthly. I was reminded of Professor Tidwell's Serengeti films.

We stopped at the outfitter in Terlingua where Grady had booked our trip. After checking in with our guide, Leon, we had a sandwich and boarded the shuttle to the river. After the cursory lecture on safety rules, we all buckled our life vests and pushed off. With the exception of the occasional stretch of rapids, the emerald water flowed gently through the precipitous canyon walls of limestone. "I've got to pee," I announced after an hour into the trip. It would've taken an independent panel of judges to determine who laughed loudest. Leon definitely laughed longest.

"Well that's good information to have," he said. "We'll stop just around the bend at the springs if that's ok."

No sooner than I had hopped out of the raft and rounded a large boulder to pull my shorts down, a large covey of Montezuma quail rose noisily out of the grass. Oblivious to the fact that my shorts were still lying on the ground, I squealed and ran from behind the boulder. Once my heart stopped pounding, I took my relief in plain view and calmly recovered my pants. Grady and Leon laughed uncontrollably.

"Laugh all you want but don't say a word," I would announce. I recalled the bidet and TIII in Baton Rouge.

Having made their way from some ancient volcanic abyss, geothermal springs periodically fed the Rio Grande. Makeshift bathing areas were bordered by large rocks that pooled the water before it gently washed into the river. We sat and talked and laughed while alternating between the hot water of the springs and the cool wash of the river. I was skipping stones when I heard Leon. "She's something else, Mr. Dalton."

"Yes, sir. She is that." Grady would agree. I recalled what had been written in the front of the leather bound journal I had been given. It was then that I knew.

Grady had rented us a yurt for the night. Our float trip concluded, we showered at the park bathhouse and went back to the campsite to have dinner. We grilled hotdogs and drank beer. Grady kept reminding me of how funny I looked standing bare-assed with my hands on my hips demanding that he and Leon *not say a word.* As the afternoon waned, we loaded some supplies into the jeep and went for a drive. The light absorbed by the stratus clouds had been refracted and re-interpreted by the atmosphere. They had turned orange and pink from the sun, purple from the hills and canyons, saffron and amber from the buttes. One lone, snowy-white cumulus cloud was uniquely out of place and a crescent moon had begun to rise. The blue and white wildflowers and the yellow blooms of the prickly pear struggled to hold their color in the diminishing light. Hoodoos rose like the spires of some ancient church and cast long shadows. We had gone off the main road and soon reached an isolated spot. We unloaded some folding chairs and blankets along with a couple of lanterns. Grady had brought along a small cooler with some beer. I manned the foot pump and inflated the air mattress. I smiled inside and thought of Mitchell. We sat and talked at length as the sun set beyond the mesa. As I had told Grady of my life experience, so he told me of his.

His family had acquired large tracts of cheap land during the mid-1800s. Cotton and cattle farming was lucrative and the Daltons made the most of it. They were also fortunate in owning tracts of land that were strategic to the booming railroad industry. Rather than selling these tracts of land, the family negotiated ninety-nine-year leases with the railroads allowing them to traverse their land unencumbered. Cinnabar mining in the area around Terlingua was an economic boon in the early 1900s and the family once again profited from lease agreements. Despite their wealth, the children and grandchildren of the Dalton clan grew up grounded in an agrarian lifestyle. Opportunities in the family holdings were earned on merit and interest. Over the years, the family holdings diversified into various facets. Those who could convince governing boards, financiers, and familial partners were given a green light for diversification. Others assumed varying roles in existing interests. Grady's responsibilities were The Hill Country Cattleman's Club and the Los Brazos Hat Company. He went on to explain that he also served as a project manager on real estate development projects but that none of it really interested him.

"What do you really want to do?" I asked.

"I'm not at all certain," he would reply.

We were from very different worlds but I knew that we would be paired. After some time, Grady said, "I want you to see something."

"Here. I want you to put these sunglasses on for a few minutes," he said.

Bewildered, I strained to watch as he took a length of thick rope and used it to carefully circle the ground around the site. "Snakes will not crawl over a rope," he said. I made sure I was on the inside of the circle.

"This is getting a little weird Grady. Ropes, snakes, *and* sunglasses?" I protested.

"Just for a few minutes," he countered.

I obliged and sat quietly while he stirred around extinguishing the lanterns. He led me over to the air mattress and had me lie down. He sat in one of the folding chairs.

"Now it's really weird. I'm lying alone on the air mattress and you're sitting in a folding chair," I laughed.

After a few minutes, he said, "Take off the sunglasses but don't say anything,"

I shivered. Every hair on my body stood on end. I heard nothing. I felt as though I might float away. I had never seen so many points of light. The indigo sky was marked by an enormous diagonal swath of stars being held in place by web-like fields of light that resembled clouds of purple and gray, their edges a pale pink. The frequency at which the meteors streaked overhead was almost frightening. The nearby rocky outcrop had taken on an ethereal glow as had everything else. The barrel cacti at its base cast long shadows in the starlight and the agave appeared as pale lavender. I shivered again and raised my hand, unwilling to speak for fear that it might all go away. After some time, I swung my feet over the edge of the air mattress and sat on its edge with my feet on the ground. Head bowed and eyes closed, I was exhausted. I was unsure how long I had been lying there. When I heard the loud scream of a wildcat nearby, I jumped to my feet. I shook uncontrollably. To no avail, he wrapped his arms around me to try and stop the trembling.

"I'm not sure what I'm supposed to do," I muttered.

"Why don't you take a seat and have a beer," he cajoled.

"That's the Milky Way," he explained pointing to the sky. "During the winter, it's almost more than the eyes can bear."

He pointed out a satellite overhead and re-lit one of the lanterns. He fiddled with the dial on a little battery powered radio until he picked up XERF-AM across the river from Del Rio. "I was raised by my grandad," he resumed. "My father was busy trying to conquer the world. He was a SEAL in the Navy and when he got out, he started a private security firm. Most of his contracts had government ties and required extensive travel. Given his extended absences, it was nearly miraculous that my mother ever became pregnant with me. I didn't particularly care for living in San Antonio. I preferred being at the ranch in Marfa. My mother's disdain for the ranch was exceeded only by that for my father. I could hardly blame her for the latter. My father is not the most likable person in the world. My mother left when I was in grade school. It didn't much matter. I rarely saw her anyway. Despite his wealth, my grandad ran the ranch as though his life depended on it. Under his tutelage and that of the ranch foreman, I learned stewardship and husbandry the hard way. It was not unheard of for him to wake me up in the middle of the night to help the vet pull a breached calf. After breakfast, he would drop me miles from the house with a post hole digger, a bundle of split rail fencing, spools of barbed wire, gloves and fencing pliers to spend the day repairing fence lines. My grandparents dragged me to church on Sundays and had no tolerance for disrespectful behavior. That old man is tough as nails but I love him like no other. He got me a part-time job at Big Bend National Park when I graduated from high school. It was better than a trip to the beach in a new Corvette and he knew it. At the end of the summer, he drove this old Jeep down here and gave it to me. That night, we forded a shallow shoal on the river and drove into the desert on the Mexican side of the river and got drunk on mescal.

Grady and I became more than lovers that night in the desert. I had no idea if or how this might coalesce. I knew only what I felt. For now, that was enough. Grady had offered and I had accepted a position at Los Brazos as a marketing and design consultant. I met with various clients to promote brand awareness and advertising ideas. Slowly (and sometimes painfully) I moved the product offering more towards increasingly upscale styling. Although western hats would remain the mainstay, gentlemen's traditional dress hats proved to be lucrative. Homburgs and fedoras found great favor among the more *seasoned* clientele of West Texas. I also worked with friends in the music business as an avenue for promoting the brand. The company acted as a sponsor at regional shows to help offset the costs of production and travel for the artists. This helped small venues retain their ability to put on shows by artists (who had become more than small regional attractions) in the smaller, more intimate venues. Artists were given new offerings for their personal use. I also worked with the factory in developing an idea for a private label of my own. I worked closely with an old Mexican named Pablo at the factory. I had sworn him to secrecy and our work was usually done after hours. I had him develop hat blocks and steaming forms that went beyond the traditional scope of the wooden forms used to shape hats. The blocks, using interchangeable components, would take into account several variations of men's' head shapes. Historically, hats were shaped as either oval or long oval or wide oval. These test blocks would accommodate numerous other common head shapes. Pear, diamond, square, heart and oblong shaped heads would be used in a custom fitting program. The hats themselves would be made of felt rendered from mink pelts combined with beaver.

Grady and I traveled most weekends. I met the family members that were scattered throughout Texas. We spent a great deal of time at the ranch in Marfa where I became very close to Grady's grandfather Beau. The old man was genuinely excited that I had begun work with the family and often asked me about various projects. Grady would bring him to San Antonio for extended visits as his interest in family business interests experienced a re-birth of sorts. Mostly, it provided an excuse for him to suggest the short drive to Austin where he could hold court at The Hill Country Cattleman's Club when he was in town. At night, I'd take him out to the clubs. "When are you two going to get married?" Beau asked one such night.

Grady had gone to the restroom. I nearly choked on my taco but recovered quickly. "Well, the subject hasn't come up," I responded.

"Well, what do you think of the idea?" He pushed back.

"I was attracted to Grady the first time I met him in Gulf Shores. We get along well and enjoy each other's company," I started.

"No. I mean, what do you think about the idea of marriage in general?"

He was serious and was going to get an answer out of me no matter how uncomfortable I got. "Honestly, it scares me," I said. "I never want to lose my independence or my individuality," I continued.

"We're all dependent on something or somebody from time to time. Foolish is the one who will not accept help, ask for help, nor lend a helping hand to another person. The willingness to accept another person as an equal in a partnership means that both parties become dependent on the other. Individuality is the result of how we exercise the gift of free will. You can no more *lose* your individuality than you can change someone else by imposing your will on them," Beau said. Thankfully, he did not pursue the same conversation when Grady returned to the table. I thought about what he had said as he recounted old stories of him and his buddies driving that old jeep into Mexico with the intent of stealing the hearts of young senoritas. His proclivity for the dark-haired beauties landed him in border town jails on more than one occasion.

One Sunday afternoon in San Antonio, Grady announced that he was going to Houston on business the following day. I had to meet some buyers in Marble Falls Monday morning and suggested that Beau ride back to Austin with me that evening. His eyes lit up. "I'll call the Driskill and get a room," he would say.

"You two are trouble looking for a place to happen," Grady said.

Beau rode to Marble Falls with me that Monday. He was greeted with affection by the employees that remembered him. He visited the office and roamed the factory while I met with the buyers in the showroom. Once our business was concluded, I found Beau in the finishing area talking to Pablo. Beau had stumbled upon the prototype blocks and started asking questions. Pablo had failed miserably at playing dumb and eventually revealed the project. I stood a few feet away. Beau's back was to me as Pablo finished explaining what we had been up to.

"What the hell!" He exclaimed. "How does she expect to sell this?" he chided.

I jumped in before Pablo could say anything else. "It's an idea for a private label," I began. "If it comes to market, the hats would be produced in limited numbers and each hat would be custom fitted for the client."

"What's the name of the label and who is the owner?" He asked.

"That is confidential at this point," I replied.

Having dodged the bullet, for the time being, I explained that we needed to get back to Austin. I had agreed to work at the Cattleman's Club that afternoon but hesitated to tell Beau. He would certainly want to go to the club but I was not comfortable working while he was there. "What other ideas are you cooking up Red?" He asked on the way back to Austin.

What do you mean?"

"That private label custom hat idea has your name written all over it," he laughed.

"It's just an idea," I replied sheepishly.

"It's a damn good idea. It needs some work; never back away from an idea you're passionate about," he advised.

I dropped Beau off at my place. Professor Tidwell came over and introduced himself. He and Beau seemed to hit it off and I left to go to the Cattleman's Club. I returned a few hours later to find the two of them well on their way to becoming very drunk. Professor Tidwell had dragged out a library of black and white photos of indigenous game animals of Texas. There were blurry images of Whitetail and Mule deer, Pronghorn antelope and Rio Grande turkeys. It had never occurred to me that a Professor of Integrative Biology would be an avid hunter.

"I've always wanted a tract of land for Mule deer research," Professor Tidwell noted. Beau had nodded off to sleep. I, on the other hand, became acutely aware of the answer to the question he had posed on the drive back to Austin from Marble Falls.

Grady returned to Austin the following day and he and Beau drove back to San Antonio. It would be a couple of weeks before I saw either of them. Grady was working and Beau was busy running for the office of Mayor of Marfa, Texas. It was a quest he had been denied on six previous attempts. It was also a source of great amusement for him. Myself, I would be busy meeting with some faculty members and graduate students to help flesh out an idea that had been going through my mind. What were once random, disconnected thoughts had begun to take on a more definitive construct. I recalled Rory telling me of his plans before he left for college and how it made me feel. I now realized that my concept of a life worth living was not as discrepant as I had thought. I loved Texas and wanted to make it my home. As much as the idea of a committed relationship frightened me, I knew also that I wanted to be with Grady.

Chapter 11

A Partner

After being apart for a couple of weeks, Grady and I flew to Gulf Shores for a long weekend. Grady promised that the trip would be purely recreational and was true to his word. As a prominent investor with the Gulf Shores Development Alliance, all amenities were his for the asking. At my behest, our first stop after checking into the condominium was P.D.'s food truck.

"Do you know where a girl can get a fresh grouper sandwich?" I cried out from the back of the short line.

Looking up from her work, P.D. squealed "Holy crap! Don't you dare move Rocket! I'll be right out!"

"Rocket," Grady pondered.

"A local nickname," I explained.

She hurriedly finished up with the couple and their two small children in front of us and turned the food truck over to the young man inside. We hugged and laughed without first speaking.

"Damn it's good to see you," she exclaimed. "Mr. Dalton, it's always a pleasure to have you in Gulf Shores." She continued.

"You know each other?" I asked, glancing back and forth between two of them.

"Well, of course, we do. Mr. Dalton is one of dad's investment partners. I thought you knew," P.D. explained.

"I knew that. I just hadn't connected the dots."

"Dad insists I sit in on meetings from time to time," P.D. pointed out. "You know me though, I'm more of a *food & beverage* girl," she laughed. She whispered in my ear, "You are all he ever talks about."

The three of us sat under an umbrella that covered a picnic table and had lunch. P.D. spoke of her boyfriends, embarrassing both Grady and myself only moderately. As I began to recount my experiences of the last couple of years, Grady excused himself. "You two catch up. I'll meet you at the marina in a bit. I'm going to book us a fishing trip for tomorrow."

P.D. and I carried on, "So, you *shot* two guys!" she exclaimed.

"It wasn't like I had much choice," I explained.

"Damn girl! Then you wound up in Austin and that's where you and Grady re-connected," she observed. "I'll just be damned," P.D. said. "You know he's crazy in love with you, right?"

"It seems so. There's something missing though," I replied

"He's afraid to tell you and he's terrified to ask you to marry him."

"Why?" I asked.

"For the same reason you are Roxanne, he's afraid of rejection and commitment."

"Let's go to The Wreck," I proposed. "I could use a beer."

P.D. declined but agreed to dinner that night. I took the moped over to the marina and found Grady. I sat some distance away and watched him and thought about what Beau had said. I thought also about what P.D. had said. As he walked past me, staring down at the brochure he'd picked up, I said, "Hey, mister! Would you buy a girl something pretty to wear to dinner tonight?"

"That depends," he laughed. "Is she buying dinner?"

We both laughed and continued walking the dock. The charter boats were starting to come in and at the end of the marina sat the Sea Star. Watching the passengers disembark, plastic dolphins in hand, I couldn't help but laugh when I thought of Griff positioning that boat so that it rocked like crazy making the kids and adults heave their breakfast over the rail.

"Permission to come aboard, Captain?" I hailed. Griffin looked down from the wheelhouse and smiled, shaking his head. "I'll be right there," he shouted.

He stepped off of the boat and walked over. "If it's not the Red Rocket," he said.

"I'm not good enough to board your vessel Capt. Stanley?" I joked.

"Well, ma'am. There was a pretty good chop on the water today and a few of the passengers got a little seasick. Maybe after we clean up a bit," he laughed. "Grady," he said extending his hand. Y'all here on business or pleasure?"

"Strictly pleasure," Grady replied. "We're going fishing tomorrow."

"Excellent! Which boat?" Griffin asked.

"The Two Brothers."

"Billy and Danny Dobbins' boat. Good choice. 1947 Bertram. Beautiful boat."

"We're meeting P.D. at The Wreck for dinner. You should join us," I remarked.

"Well, I might see you guys later but I won't make dinner. I've got the dinner cruise tonight. There's a good band playing over there though," Griff pointed out.

"We'll save you a seat," I promised.

"And a dance?" Griff asked, looking back and forth between Grady and myself.

"You bet!" I said.

Grady and I returned to the hotel, changed into swimwear, and headed toward the pool. After a couple of mandatory Hemingways, we walked down to the beach.

"It's nice here," he remarked.

"It is," I agreed. "It's no place to live, though. I would wager that it's terribly lonely during the offseason."

"You're probably right," he agreed.

I picked up a shark's tooth and handed it to him. "Grady, what are you and I? I mean, if someone asks, how do you describe *us*? Our relationship." The words came stumbling out of my mouth before I could stop myself.

"Well, I've never known anyone like you. I've never spent time with anyone like you. You're smart as hell and funny. You've got a bangin' body and a bad-ass car." We both laughed. "I miss you when we're not together and when we are together, I don't want you to go."

I smiled and nodded my head. "What do you think is more difficult, a business partner or a relationship partner?" I asked.

"Business relationships are usually clearly defined. All parties work toward the goal of making a profit. I've always done well with that model. Relationships? Not so much. I was married once and failed miserably. Too many intangibles," he continued.

"Given our relationship, could you get behind a business plan with me?"

"If I had to choose one or the other, I'd rather have our personal relationship. I would not, however, discount a business idea *because* of our relationship. It would have to be more than simple dollars and cents though. I have enough business responsibilities. It would have to be something very special. It would have to be life-changing."

We went back to the condominium and showered. I was the first out and ran a brush through my hair before going out on the balcony to air dry. I was leaning against the railing wearing only a t-shirt when I heard Grady's voice. "Leon was right," he said. "You are something else." I smiled and led him back inside.

We arrived at The Wreck a little later than we had planned. The hostess led us to a table where P.D. was seated with a man she introduced only as the guitar player in the band. He excused himself almost as if on cue. "Guitar player, huh? You're moving up in the world," I laughed.

"Screw you, Rocket! At least I'm not wearing my shirt with the wrong side out," P.D. countered.

"Damnit! Touché madame," I replied.

Grady was laughing hysterically as I casually removed my shirt to turn the right side out. Before I got my shirt back on, P.D. noted, "And Mr. Dalton, you sir, should check your zipper. As a matter of fact, maybe you lovebirds should go back to your room and start all over. We do have standards in this establishment, and right now you two are stomping all over them."

A waitress showed up with a tray full of Mudslides and we toasted the day. We ordered grouper throats and smoked tuna dip. Not long after the band began to play, Griffin walked through the door. It was comfortable and it was fun. I felt connected. I remembered watching my friends in Circle City and recognizing how connected they were and how empty it made me feel. The only sense of commonality I had ever experienced died with Henry during that thunderstorm so long ago. My heart was full.

"Who's in the cardroom, P.D.?" I asked

"You and a damned cardroom! The usual bunch of cigar-smoking, lie-telling men is in the cardroom! What else would you expect?"

"I'd like to drop in," I said soberly. "I'd like to see Elian."

P.D. got up and walked across the room to the bar where she picked up a house phone.

"You don't mind I hope," I posed to Grady.

"Would it matter if I did?" he laughed.

P.D. started back toward our table and cocked her head approvingly toward the hallway that led to the cardroom.

"I won't stay long. I just want to say hello," I said.

"Don't you worry, I'll take care of this fellow for you," she said as she took Grady by the hand and walked toward the dance floor.

The doorman stood from his stool to let me in; the room was as I remembered. Griffin's father announced to the table that I was a most welcome guest. The players and I exchanged nods and I walked to the bar. "Buy a lady a drink, Mister?"

"Got some identification, ma'am?" Elian laughed.

I stood, rather than sat, at the small bar and made small talk about the game as he polished the heavy, leaded glassware. He offered me a Por Larranaga Panetela and lit it for me before handing it to me. It was a custom of Cubans and considered a show of respect and admiration. "Have you found what you were looking for," he inquired.

"I think so, yes. It's still very new," I spoke.

He nodded pensively and noted: "There is an old saying in Cuba. Lo nuevo es agradable y lo viejo es satisfactorio. It means: *what is new is pleasing and what is old is satisfying*," he quoted. We visited for a while longer. I verbalized a rough sketch of my idea.

"You have a beautiful soul and a sound mind. Trust yourself and you'll be fine. Anything worth dreaming is worth living."

I returned to find our table empty; P.D. was predictably huddled up with the guitar player near the bar but I did not see Grady. "P.D., have you seen Grady?" I asked.

"Yeah. He and Griffin walked out on the deck."

I walked out to the deck and watched from a distance. I intuitively recognized their conversation as one of a personal matter. Griffin looked dejected when he stood to leave the umbrella-covered table. "I'm happy for you Roxanne. He's a good man," he would say as he passed.

"What was that all about," I asked Grady.

"It would seem that Griffin is enamored of you."

"That's just the alcohol talking," I laughed.

"No. He went on and on about the summer you were here and how he'd always hoped to see you again and how he never wanted to be without you and that if he ever saw you again he would tell you how he felt. It was a little uncomfortable."

"What did you say, Grady?"

"I told him that you and I were in a relationship and that I felt the same way. He was embarrassed for not knowing or recognizing it."

"Well, he'll grow out of it. He'll have to." It was all that I could think to say.

Reminded that we had a 05:00 appointment with the Two Brothers, Grady and I returned to the condominium. I felt as though I had just fallen asleep when Grady crowed the day, "Rise and shine Rocket! We're going fishing!" he exclaimed as he opened the drapery that covered the sliding glass door that led to the balcony.

"Damnit Grady, it's still dark!" I cried.

"It is four o'clock in the morning, Roxanne. What would you expect?"

"I would expect most folks to be asleep and if you keep on whooping and hollering they'll all be awake."

"Get dressed and run a brush through your hair. You look like a rooster. I'll let you buy breakfast," he laughed.

"A rooster? You'll starve after that comment!" I scowled. I took one look in the mirror and opted for a hat rather than an attempt to make sense of the hair on my head. We dressed and drove to a nearby all-night breakfast joint for waffles, eggs, and copious amounts of coffee. We drove to the marina and walked down to the Two Brothers slip where we noticed that one of the Dobbins brothers was in the engine housing, and the other had a somewhat concerned look on his face.

"Everything ok?" Grady inquired.

"Yes, sir. Just finishing up. We were late getting in and needed to change a couple of filters is all. Y'all ready to go fishing?"

"Does a rooster crow the day?" I countered. I stepped gingerly onto the boat. "That's an inside joke guys," I said and looked back at Grady.

~ 287 ~

Dawn broke as we made our way out of the no wake zone and into the gulf. Capt. Billy was on the flybridge and Danny was making ready the fishing gear. We watched as he explained the differences between the braided line and the monofilament leader, how the two were joined and the size and type of hooks and the different types of reels. "We found amberjack schooling around an artificial reef not far from here yesterday. Big fish. 80-100 pounds. We'll use these once we get there. Those in the rod holders now are much lighter. We'll use them to start trolling for Mahi and small blackfin tuna in a few minutes."

Capt. Billy backed down on the throttle and called down. "There's a huge bed of floating grass out here. Let's get those bucktail jigs in the water and see what happens."

"Hang on, this could get a little crazy," Danny explained. "Roxanne, you here and Grady, you over there."

Danny opened the bail on the large spinning reels and cast the lures into the water. The two were set at different lengths behind the boat to help avoid tangling the lines. After a few minutes, Billy cried out. "Sailfish! Starboard side!"

"Grady, get your line in! Quick," Danny instructed.

Grady began to reel furiously. Danny tended to me. "You'll know if he takes it," he explained. "When he does, crank the reel two turns and lean back quick and hard three times." Like some crazed cartoon character, he was talking fast and maniacally demonstrating what he was talking about. Just as suddenly, there was a hard thump on the rod and the line began screaming off of the reel. "Reel! Reel! Reel!" he shouted. I cranked the reel and leaned back hard into the chair. "Just hold him," Danny explained. "When he stops running, we'll work on getting some of the line back."

Billy had maneuvered us away from the bed of grass to avoid getting tangled. Grady was busy taking photographs. My shoulders and legs burned from the strain. My opponent and I seemed to have reached an impasse when Danny started coaching me again. "Ok. I want you to ease the rod tip down slowly and crank the reel as you go." I repeated the move over and over, each time gaining some of the line back onto the reel. My arms now burned as my shoulders and legs.

"You ok Rocket?" Grady asked. "You need a break? Want me to take it for a minute?"

"No!"

Time and again the fish would run, taking back the line I had painfully recovered until finally, I heard Billy cry out from the flybridge, "Thirty feet! Get the gaff! Damn! He's lit up like a bar sign!"

Just then, the fish breached. It hung in the air for what seemed like an eternity. The fish contorted its body, slashing its bill at the invisible line that held it. The neon blue and amber lateral lines, the vertical stripes, and the silver belly all burned indelibly in my mind. When the great fish finally hit the water, the line went slack. The fish was gone. The sudden lack of resistance caused me to slam back into my chair. I couldn't hear anything. All of my senses were focused on that image of the fish. Everything appeared to be moving in slow motion. I turned and saw that Grady and Danny were both shaking their heads with looks of great anguish. Captain Billy, up in the flybridge, appeared similarly sullen. Slowly, my senses returned and I began to shout and dance about the deck. I clambered up the ladder to the flybridge and hugged Capt. Billy. I came back down and grabbed three beers out of the large cooler. "Drinks on me boys!" I shouted. "That was awesome! Grady, did you see that? Holy crap!"

"I'm sorry we lost that fish," Danny chagrined.

"What the hell would I have done with it? Put a leash on it and take him for a walk?" I laughed.

The men all looked at each other and began to laugh. I asked Capt. Billy to put on some music. Alone, with my eyes closed, I danced to Gasoline Alley.

Chapter 12

Dark Skies Lodge

After our trip to Gulf Shores, I was genuinely excited to be back in Austin. So much so that I had to sit down and make a *to-do* list. Between working at the Cattleman's Club, and my responsibilities with Los Brazos, it started to look a little overwhelming. I remembered what Rory had told me about gathering the pecans. "Just break it up into little pieces Roxanne," I repeated. Fortunately, the starting point for my idea resided right outside the door of my little carriage house. I convinced myself that dropping in on Professor Tidwell and his cronies one afternoon during a card game would be an opportune setting for me to begin. I knew them all and I was always welcomed to the card game. Being nervous should not be a consideration. Then it occurred to me that I was fixing to engage a group of men in a conversation regarding a matter of which I had little knowledge. I remembered what Beau had said about independence.

"What's the matter with you, Roxanne? You might just as well hand over all of your money and save yourself the misery of losing one hand after another!" Dr. Harralson observed.

"I'm a little distracted," I began. "I need some help."

Everyone at the table immediately folded their hand.

"Are you in trouble?"

"Do you need money"

"Are you leaving us?" The questions came in rapid succession. This one prompted a full-on belly laugh.

"No, no and HELL NO," I laughed. "I have an idea that needs some help. I'm betting the limit that you gentlemen can provide some answers and direction if you're willing."

I had their attention. I stood from the table. "Professor Tidwell, do you think the University would be interested in having access to a large tract of land for wildlife biology research?"

He sat a little more upright. "Well, from a personal standpoint, I'd be interested. The University of Texas has long been a benefactor of land grants and donations. It's a mutually beneficial relationship. Access to and specific use of those resources is handled through the Board of Regents. Generally speaking, by the time the *powers that be* are finished slicing up the pie, peons like us have little to say with regard to their use," he replied.

"Here's what I need for now," I began. "I need a legal agreement for presentation purposes. Something that outlines an arrangement between the landowner and the University. It need not be very specific and for the time being, the name of the property owner will not be used. I want you to have it drawn up so that The Board of Regents will know that its purpose is for wildlife biology research only. I want the access and use of the property to be determined by your department and the landowner."

"Roxanne, funding for research and having resources for field studies are two very different things. You could gain access to the entire Amazon Basin for biological research and it would be useless without funding," Dr. Harralson pointed out.

"Well, we'll have to cross that bridge when we get to it. There's one other thing. I need some information on state and/or federal tax benefits, if any, that the landowner might realize from the agreement. When do think you can have this ready?" I asked.

Dr. Stanford made a point, "A Land Use Agreement is quite common and nearly generic. That's easy enough to get. You audited some classes at the Law School, Roxanne. If it's just for presentation purposes, you should be able to get a copy at the Law Library. I'll look at the tax relief potential and see what I can turn up. Give me until the end of the week."

"Land Use Agreement," I repeated as I jotted it down. "Great, thanks."

"If the first few hurdles can be cleared, this will be a huge undertaking. The project will require a great deal of input, energy, participation, and money from numerous sources. I'd like for all of you to be a part of it," I concluded. "One more thing. For the time being, this all needs to be held in confidence."

The following day, I dropped by the Graduate Assistants' office at the McCombs School of Business. I was fortunate to find exactly who I was looking for. I had taken

Marketing at the Business School and the graduate assistant for the class was Darrell Harper. He was socially awkward but I always went out of my way to be nice to him. He reminded me of Taylor at Roebuck Academy. When asked, and after dropping the books he was carrying, I had Darrell agree to meet me at a sandwich shop off campus later that afternoon.

"I have a business idea that needs some research work," I began. "Honestly, I don't know how simple or how complex it might be to mine the information I'm looking for. I can't pay you. I thought, however, that it might be something that you or someone you know could use as part of a graduate thesis."

"I might be able to help. What kind of information are you looking for?" Darrell asked.

"My idea is to build and operate a multi-use facility near Marfa. Please keep this confidential Darrell. The centerpiece would be a large lodge. The building itself would serve, for the most part, as an events venue. The facility would be a location for business meetings, reunions, conferences, conventions, weddings, and various types of receptions. It would also serve as a facility for flourishing musicians and artists to showcase their talents. The property itself will be developed and promoted as *the* premier trophy hunting experience in West Texas. In season, the lodge will host guests of the property for meals and entertainment and would serve as a central point for the guests to share their experiences. I have a few secondary ideas as well," I stated.

Darrell sat staring at me before he spoke. "What is it that you need from me?"

"I need a feasibility study. I need something that will point toward a real demand for such a facility. I need direction on how to promote a world-class trophy hunting experience and what kind of demand it would attract. I need numbers regarding existing availability and demand in the West Texas geographic region for 1st class event facilities," I explained.

"That's quite a list, Roxanne."

"Some of my friends call me Rocket," I replied. It did not get the response I was hoping for.

"Roxanne, what you are asking for is more than just an opinion or some *off-the-shelf* demographics profile. This sort of research takes some considerable time and effort. Time isn't something that I have much of," he said.

"I understand." It was all that I could say.

"I'll tell you what. I'll make a list of initial items to research and point you in the right direction. You provide the basics and I'll interpret what you come up with. Deal?"

"Ok. I can do that. Where and how do I start?"

"Go to the DNR office and request a list of full-service hunting outfitters. Then go to the Chamber of Commerce and inquire about the conference centers. Let them know what you are considering. Call all of the resources they refer you to. Ask for prices, service offerings, locations, availability, and references."

"Anything else," I asked.

"Yes. Take notes. Come find me when you have something to work with," he suggested.

"Darrell, what's DNR stand for?" I asked.

"Department of Natural Resources," he smiled.

I was late for work at Hill Country Cattleman's Club that afternoon. Not that it mattered much. I worked for tips and the only one dinged if I didn't work was me. It didn't hurt that I was in a relationship with the owner either. That particular day, however, I was a little surprised to see Beau Dalton in attendance. His cronies were ribbing him about running for Mayor of Marfa again.

I moved in to rescue him. "You could use a shave, old man," I announced.

Beau rubbed his chin gingerly and replied, "I believe you're right, young lady. Know where I can get one?" He laughed.

"Come on back and I'll see what I can do," I said.

Beau settled into the barber's chair and I took a hot towel from the autoclave. I wrapped his face to soften his beard while I brushed up some shaving lather. After removing the towel, I spread the warm lather over his face. I began to sharpen the razor on the cordovan strop.

"I wasn't expecting to see you today," I commented casually. "You got a date tonight?"

"Only if you don't have any plans," he hinted coyly.

"Well, there's a show at the Armadillo. Los Brazos is sponsoring. Interested?"

"Hell yeah," he said. "I'd like that. I hear sales are way up since you came on board. You've done a helluva job over there." He commented.

"I don't have much sense about stuff like that Beau. I'm good with ideas. Accounting ledgers and balance sheets, not so much." I frowned.

"Don't sell yourself short Roxanne. Nobody can do it all," he replied.

I went about my work. I knew the old man had a good reason for being in Austin and that he would tell me when he was ready. I finished his face and cleaned him up. I took another towel from the autoclave to use on his neck.

"You know, you and Grady are a lot alike," he began. "He's short on ideas but good with numbers and the such. You are just the opposite."

"Conversely similar," I implied.

"If you say so. He's crazy about you. You know that," Beau observed.

"Yeah. I'm kinda stuck on him too," I replied.

"I'm kinda worried about something though," he continued.

I felt like I'd been kicked in the gut. I thought I was fixing to get a lecture about some poor little girl from nowhere breaking his grandson's heart and making off with the family fortune or something. "Yeah? What would that be?" I asked with a stiff upper lip.

"Grady is a country boy at heart Roxanne. He'll be the first one to tell you that none of his work interests him much. I mean, everybody has to work, right? I just wish he could find something that he really loves doing. Do you know what I'm talking about?"

I brushed the old man off with talc. "You let me worry about that, Beau. I'll pick you up at the Driskill around eight. Ok?"

"No need. Tidwell is putting me up for the night. I stopped by there earlier looking for you. I like that guy. He's good people. Maybe he'll come with us tonight. I'll see you back at your place."

I was barely halfway out of the car door when Professor Tidwell walked up. "We need to talk. This Land Use Agreement is more than just an altruistic act. We all know that. It occurred to me this afternoon, however, that the landowner is Beau Dalton and that he knows nothing about it. Why?"

"Where is he?" I asked.

"He's inside taking a shower."

"The idea is nowhere near ready to present to Beau, Professor Tidwell. The Land Use Agreement and your research are two of many fundamental elements that will determine whether any of this is a sound business idea or not. You and the others were the first people to know anything about this. I didn't disclose any more than I did because it's no more than an idea at this point. If you'll keep it to yourself until I can see everything more clearly, I'll tell you this much. My hope is that your research will help in developing a world-class trophy hunting experience. My hope is that studies in genetics, birth rates, mortality, nutrition, and population balance between different species, especially predators, will assist in developing a game management plan like none other. That being said, can you put something together for me by next Friday?"

"Well, I'll just be damned. If that is the *small* part of your plan, I'm not so sure my pea brain can handle the *big* part. Deal me in!" he exclaimed.

Just then, Beau called out from an upstairs window he had opened. "Hey! You two gonna shower and change clothes or go like you are?"

"Give me ten minutes old man!"

"Yeah. I"ll show you an *old man*," Beau laughed back.

"Not a word. Ok?" I posed to Professor Tidwell. He held his index finger up to his clenched lips.

I took them both through the rear entrance reserved for performers, crew, and staff at the Armadillo. Beau let Professor Tidwell know that he was a seasoned veteran at these events. He'd call out by name to performers that he recognized, or had previously met, and made sure that he introduced them to Professor Tidwell who was duly impressed. The two of them were not as dissimilar as I would have imagined.

Eddie Wilson came for me when it was time for the show to begin. As the designated brand ambassador for the Los Brazos Hat Company which sponsored the event, it was my responsibility to go onstage and make announcements. It was a songwriter's showcase for local and regional writers and performers to garner exposure, and I would be busy going on and off stage to make announcements for most of the evening. This left Beau and Professor Tidwell alone to roam the backstage area. This visual image caused a moderate degree of consternation on my part but they proved to be harmless for the most part.

During one of the introductions, I saw Darrell Harper in the audience. Afterward, I walked to the table where he was seated and took him in tow. We made our way to the backstage area and found Beau and Professor Tidwell talking with Billy Joe Shaver. "Hey Rocket! Beau tells me you have a new line of custom hats," he exclaimed.

"Rocket?" Professor Tidwell asked.

"It's a nickname," Beau explained.

"Working on it. You want me to let you know when the label is ready?"

"Why hell yeah," he said excitedly.

"And I'm gonna take you up on that offer to go hunting, Beau. I'll see y'all later," Billy Joe remarked. I looked at Professor Tidwell and rolled my eyes while shaking my head. His expression was one of complete innocence. Darrell appeared starstruck.

"I'll come to your office Tuesday if that's ok," I said to Darrell.

"Yes, ma'am. That will be fine. Anytime is fine," he said.

As part of my due diligence, I had made two questionnaires. One was to be used for interviewing outfitters and the other for interviewing persons who had agreed to act as referrals. The most important question the outfitters were asked to address was what they considered to be *unique* about their operation while the referrals were asked what they found unique about their *experience*. The same questions were posed to event facilities that hosted business meetings, conferences, and social gatherings. It quickly became apparent that my notion of a unique, world-class experience far exceeded those of the parties I polled.

When I met with Darrell on Tuesday, I was less than surprised to find that his interest in my project had spiked. It would seem that *a good time* failed miserably in describing his experience at the Armadillo and the ensuing debauchery. He had done some research of his own, and his findings were similar to mine.

"What else can I do to help?" he asked

"Would you be willing to put this together in a format suitable for presentation?" I asked.

"You bet! Stop by Friday," he replied

I went to change clothes before a quick trip to Marble Falls and was fortunate in seeing Professor Tidwell was home. He and his cohorts were holed up in the library when I walked in.

"What are you outlaws up to?" I asked.

Dr. Harralson began to speak. "Tidwell gave us the details of your plan. We're all in. We've been working on this all weekend. We've solicited some outside input from Texas A&M also. We think that a collaborative effort with their Wildlife Management & Fisheries Department will be the icing on the cake. We believe that in a period of...."

"Guys! I'm sorry to interrupt but I have to go to Marble Falls for a business meeting. Can I count on you to have something to present next week? Grady and Beau will be here and I want to put this on the table for them to have a look at."

"We'll be ready," they replied in unison.

I drove to Marble Falls to meet with Pablo at Los Brazos Hat. He had been working with the felting department to develop a workable blend of mink and beaver for the private label line of hats. His work on the various hat blocks and the felting process was a labor of love for the old man. He took great pride in knowing that I had entrusted him to develop my idea. He had brought in co-workers from the felting department and finishing departments as well. They explained the nuances of working with the felt, the dyeing process, and finishing. Finally, Pablo's son Enrique came into the showroom with a hatbox. The box was black with red trim and in the center was the likeness of a rooster. I opened the box and took the hat out. It was a copper color that seemingly matched my hair color. I smiled and looked over at Pablo.

"The felt holds dye very well, but it did take some time to get the color right," he smiled.

The grosgrain silk hatband was embellished with a small, enameled hat pin of a fighting cock. I put the hat on and looked in the mirror. True to my personal taste, it was a classic fedora with a teardrop crown and pinched front crease. The fit was perfect, and the finish was impeccable. It looked and felt very expensive. I took it off and looked inside. The leather sweatband was embossed with gold ink: Custom Made for Roxanne Benefield. The silk hat liner was designed with a silkscreen image of a rooster. Arched across the top of the rooster was the logo: Rooster Hat Company, and at the bottom: The Cock of the Walk. Enrique did the artwork and had a vendor produce samples for both the hat box and liners.

"I cannot tell you all how thrilled I am. This is absolutely perfect. This is the beginning of a very special line of hats. I'm trusting you to make every hat as perfect as this one. I applaud you. I'll not forget your efforts." I began clapping my hands and continued until they all joined in.

Thursday, I met with a contractor in San Marcos. Dan Nelson had been referred by a faculty member at the School of Architecture by way of a referral from one of Dr. Stanford's graduate assistants. To the best of my ability, I explained my vision of the lodge. It was to be a large, timber frame and stone structure. The centerpiece of the great room was to be a 360° fireplace of flat creek stone. There was to be a dining hall and kitchen, a gallery, business office, three conference rooms, and a trophy room. Staircases on both ends of the great room would lead upstairs to the six suites that would accommodate overnight guests. Dan was gracious in agreeing to provide photos of his work, referrals, and a floorplan. He also agreed to participate in the presentation.

As I went through my mental checklist during the drive back to Austin, I was stricken by the sudden realization that I had overlooked what was most likely the paramount element of the plan. I had nothing to demonstrate the costs or income potential of the project. I stopped the car at a truck stop and alternately cursed and cried; all the while, I pounded on the steering wheel of the Rambler.

I eventually gathered my wits and continued toward Austin. When I got home, I found the three amigos huddled in Professor Tidwell's library outlining their presentation. Assignation of the various tasks was made and a timeline for completion was put forth. It was at that moment I realized that I had garnered the efforts, cooperation, and enthusiasm of a group of people that believed in me. To simply roll over and play dead because I was feeling inadequate would be a disservice to us all. My pity party having concluded, I went to work at The Hill Country Cattleman's Club. It was by chance that I met a noted record producer named Billy

Sherrill that evening. When he told me that he was scouting talent for his record label, I mentioned the names of some of Austin's local talent base. I also told him the names of the clubs where he might find what he was looking for.

I blurted out a question without knowing why. "What does it take to make a hit record?"

Mr. Sherrill laughed and began to explain, "No one knows what makes a *hit* record but making *a* record involves a lot of unique ingredients. It begins with an idea for a song. A song might be about a jilted lover, a night on the town, or the death of a loved one. The subjects are unlimited. The *idea* usually, but not always, comes from a songwriter. Once the lyrics are written, an accompanying melody is worked out. This part might, or might not, come from a source other than the writer. The songwriter is usually under a publishing contract that takes ownership of the material and decides what to do with it. A song might sit untouched for years before ever being recorded. Record label publicists do what they can to promote material for recording purposes. A great number of *recording artists* have no talent for writing songs; their talent is singing. Matching a song with a singer is a hit and miss proposition. Some artists choose the music they record where others are mandated to record what their record label dictates. Once a song and a vocalist are matched, a recording is made. A producer schedules time with a recording studio and assembles a team of musicians and engineers to record the song. It's the producer's job to bring together all of these elements to record the song the way he thinks it sounds best. The songwriter that scratched the lyrics on a cocktail napkin and matched a three-chord melody to it might scarcely recognize the finished product. Of course, nearly all of this is subject to no strict rules. The melody might very well come before the lyrics and the songwriter might actually be the one that records the song. A recording artist might have a stipulation in his contract that allows him to choose is own material. The variables are unlimited."

"Good God! How the hell does anything get accomplished with that many cooks in the kitchen?" I exclaimed.

"It begins and ends with an idea for a song and someone to put all of the pieces together," he explained. "A three-minute song is a huge undertaking that no one can do alone. I don't play guitar, sing, or write but give me a good song and free reign in a studio and I'll make you a million bucks."

During the week preceding the presentation, I became ill. Nauseous and tired, I lacked any semblance of an appetite and I was void of energy. Once I found it hard to focus, I made a doctor's appointment. He examined me, recorded my vital signs and drew blood for some lab work. He asked a lot of questions about my medical history and my family's medical history. I explained that I had never been sick or injured and except for vaccinations required by the school board, I had never seen a doctor.

"Ms. Benefield, if I had to make a guess I'd say you are pregnant. The blood work will be back in a few days and we'll know for sure. Until then, try to eat soft foods and if you get tired, stop what you are doing and rest," he stated nonchalantly.

Having regained my senses, for the time being, I stopped myself short of arguing his pre-mature diagnosis. Afterall, it made perfectly good sense.

I had made Beau and Grady aware of the fact that I had been researching a project that I wanted to discuss with

~ 313 ~

them. It wasn't the sort of thing to casually bring up over tacos and beer. I had arranged for all of the participants to meet at Professor Tidwell's on Friday afternoon. Afterward, we would all go out for dinner. The call from the doctor's office came as everyone was arriving. I was indeed pregnant. After hanging up the phone, I stood in the doorway and looked across the courtyard. A feeling of immense gratification welled up inside of me when Grady and Beau both looked my way and smiled. I led the participants into the library and my vision of Dark Skies Lodge was laid bare.

I opened by recounting Billy Sherrill's description of how to make a record. "That being said, I'd like to thank everyone who has selflessly joined me in making this presentation," I began.

"Dark Skies Lodge would be a multi-use facility. As it's foundation, the operation will offer a world-class trophy hunting experience for sportsmen around the world. Through a cooperative effort with the University of Texas and Texas A&M, academic consultants will develop a game management plan based on genetics, nutrition, predator-to-prey ratios, and conservation focused on desert mule deer, elk, pronghorn, and desert bighorn sheep. Aside from the big game, Rio Grande turkey and varmint hunting will be available as well. As a full-service outfitter, Dark Skies Lodge and its staff will offer an experience of unparalleled amenities and quality. Hunting will be permitted in a regulated manner designed to maintain healthy populations of trophy animals. Interested parties will pay to be part of a lottery system that will determine who will be allowed to hunt. Guides will designate which animals, if any, will be taken by the hunters. In addition to traditional firearms hunts, Dark Skies Lodge will offer unique, alternative hunts. Photo safaris, catch and release hunts, and non-lethal weapons hunts will challenge guests to stalk animals in their natural habitat in an effort to gain extreme proximity. These non-lethal hunt offerings will create a new market of enthusiasts. These hunts will use archery equipment that has no arrowheads and air rifles that shoot paint-filled pellets. Lastly, when occasions arise that field studies requiring blood and tissue sample collections, select guests will have the opportunity to accompany research teams on hunts with tranquilizer equipment. Professor Tidwell and his group will explain their theories and management ideas. Their efforts will assure guests that the quality of their experience will be of the highest order."

As I walked to my seat, I took stock of the expression on the faces of the participants. I had clearly gotten their attention. No one in the room had been made privy to all of these details prior to my speaking. Professor Tidwell's group had prepared overhead slides that pointed to the premise that genetics and nutrition were the fundamental elements of producing trophy animals.

"Scrawny, undernourished animals with less than impressive attributes do not produce offspring that grow up to be premium examples of their species," he concluded.

"I was about to give up on you Tidwell," Beau laughed. "THAT I can understand!"

Dr. Harralson took the hint from this when it was his turn. He showed numbers that demonstrated he had done his homework while incorporating a bare-bones explanation of how to focus only on pertinent ingredients. "There would be no need to work for controlling predator populations unless there is an identifiable imbalance," he explained. "Similarly, you would not want to invite folks to a turkey hunt if there are no turkeys." Including my building contractor from San Marcos, everyone nodded in agreement.

"A Land Use Agreement with the University of Texas System and the Board of Regents provides a considerable number of opportunities," Dr. Stanford began. "We've had only a limited time to look at this, but it is clear that there are potential tax advantages that property owners can claim as part of conservation easements and other legal instruments. The Texas Constitution and Tax Code stipulates guidelines for special use appraisals for land used to manage wildlife. This potentially lowers the tax considerations for the property owner. Again, we would have to take a closer look at this but the preliminary findings are very promising."

It was taking considerably longer than I originally anticipated so I suggested a break. "Who needs a break?" I asked

"I need a Lone Star beer," Beau crowed.

"I just happen to have one," Professor Tidwell proffered.

I was cautious to minimize the break and drew the participants focus back to the task at hand. "Come on, guys, I'm getting hungry," I said.

"Before we get any further down this road, I have a question," Beau said. "Who are we going to sell this to?" I smiled in my mind. He was sold on the idea.

"We could promote Dark Skies to outdoor magazine publishers, hunting equipment manufacturers and distributors, university alumni, politicians, and established business contacts. There are a lot of avenues available."

"Roxanne, where would this operation be based?" Grady asked.

All eyes were on me but the answer came from Beau Dalton. "Marfa," he stated with a look of supreme satisfaction on his face. I smiled as well.

"There's much more. As I stated earlier, the lodge itself would serve as a multi-use events facility. Marfa, Texas is blossoming as a destination for artists. The lodge would host gallery shows as well as musical entertainment provided by budding artists anxious to gain exposure. Our acquaintances in the music industry might receive special consideration for facility usage in exchange for private performances. In addition, business conferences, receptions, private parties, reunions, and eco-tourists can all be accommodated. Dan Nelson will help explain my vision of the lodge."

"Are you Ben Nelson's son?" Beau asked.

"Yes, sir," he replied.

"I'm quite familiar with your work. I know your dad. Do you have a floor plan?"

As Dan Nelson presented his floor plan, I passed around a book of photos depicting structures similar to what I had envisioned. The meeting no longer required my direction. It had taken on an agenda of its own. Finally, Beau interrupted the sidebar conversations. "What else do you have planned Roxanne?"

All eyes were again on me. "A pecan grove. I want a pecan grove," I started. The room grew quiet. "Once established, pecan trees require little maintenance and yield an excellent cash crop. I found my way here with the help of a little pecan grove in Alabama and I'd like to have a grove for my children to operate. I want to make Texas my home. I left a life that was hardly worth living to make a life worth celebrating. I hope this is it."

"Well I must say, I am duly impressed. I commend you all for your efforts. It's a lot to mull over and I think dinner would be a good place to start," Grady said.

"Wait just a damn minute," Beau protested. "I think I missed something. What children are you talking about?"

Again, the room grew silent and all eyes cast in my direction. "Your great-grandchildren, of course," I remarked. "I'm pregnant."

As the others sat dumbfounded, a chuckle rose from Grady. It grew into a laugh and crescendoed, finally, as a joyous celebration with him twirling me around in circles while the others applauded. While they talked among themselves, Grady and I put a record on the turntable. "You better check on the old man," he said. "I think he's shell-shocked."

"May I have his dance, sir?" I asked. A tear in his eye, Beau Dalton stood and we danced to Somewhere Over The Rainbow.

Later that night, the phone in the cottage house rang. It was Charlie Hardwick. Tom Gentry was dying and asked to see me. I felt compelled to drive but Grady insisted that I fly. I rented a car at the airport and drove to Charlie and Cynthia's house. My heart in Texas, I still felt as though I was returning home. Cynthia had a vacant look with which I was unfamiliar. Charlie explained that her mental condition had deteriorated and the medications kept her from being suicidal. She never got over Jessica's death. My journals provided some solace over the years, but she sometimes failed to realize that it was not Jessica's writing.

We had a quiet dinner and I drove to the nursing home. Tom Gentry was sleeping peacefully when I entered his room. A pedestal fan circulated the air. A small black and white television was on but the volume was turned down too low to hear. A serving tray with food sat untouched next to the bed. Underneath the bedside table was a stack of my journals. I sat quietly; I wasn't sure what, if anything, I should do. I was staring blankly at the television when Tom spoke.

"Well, ain't you a sight fo' sore eyes," he grinned.

I took his hand. I was momentarily unable to speak. "I see you got some of my journals," I finally said.

"I sho' did. Mr. Harley reads 'em to me mostly. I learnt to read a little fo' myself but I'm kinda slow at it," he explained. "Thays sumpin' under the bed I want you to have."

I started to talk but he stopped me. "I ain't got time to argue. Reach up under there and git it out," he pleaded.

It was that damned old guitar. I sat shaking my head.

"It's all I got and I want you to have it. That ol' git'tar is worth a right smart uh money if you have a mind to sell it. Thays a fellow up in Nashville kin tell you all about it. Thays a bunch of papers in the case that tells the story of where it's been and how it got here. You kin do whatever you want wit' it…it's yores now."

We spoke quietly for a while. I could tell he was in great pain, and that his breathing was growing shallow. "I want you to do one thang fo' me," Tom begged. "Carry my ashes back home with you. Scatter 'em out under dem stars. I'd like that." I assured him that I would.

"I been colorblind my 'ho life." He continued. " All I ever seen was gray or white or black. Ever'thang looked like shadows. First time I seen you, I seen you had red hair and green eyes. You had on a yellow shirt and white sneakers. The back pocket of yo' britches had a little red tag. "It's the damndest thing. Yous all I ever seen in color."

A meteor streaking across the not yet dark sky caught my eye. When I looked back, Tom Gentry's eyes had shut for the final time. He was gone.

Epilogue

That night, I slept in the loft of the barn at the Hardwick's. I heard the owls calling from opposing sides of the property. I returned to Texas, and from the top of a cliff in the Chisos Mountains during the Leonids meteor shower, I loosed Tom Gentry's ashes into the wind. Grady and I watched over every detail of the Dark Skies Lodge project that would become our life's work. The first event to be held at the lodge was a non-traditional wedding ceremony for Grady and I. Our son, Gentry Beauregard Dalton was two years old by then. That same year, following numerous failed attempts, Beau Dalton was elected Mayor of Marfa, Texas.

77674977R00194

Made in the USA
Middletown, DE
25 June 2018